SAPPHIRE

By the same author

THE MARQUIS AND MISS JONES
BEAU BARRON'S LADY
REGENCY ROGUE
THE MICHAELMAS TREE
THE LOVING HIGHWAYMAN
EMERALD
MIDSUMMER-MORNING
PEARL
RUBY

SAPPHIRE

Helen Ashfield

St. Martin's Press
New York

Library of Congress Cataloging in Publication Data

Bennetts, Pamela.
    Sapphire.

    I. Title.
PR6052.E533S37   1986   823'.914   85-25054
ISBN 0-312-69962-X

First published in Great Britain by Robert Hale Limited.

10 9 8 7 6 5 4 3 2

ACKNOWLEDGEMENTS.

I owe a great debt of gratitude to the following authors
for without their scholarship this novel could not have
been written:

The Beginnings of Industrial Britain	S. D. Chapman & J. D. Chambers.
Human Documents of the Industrial Revolution in Britain	E. Royston Pike.
The Past at Work	Anthony Burton.
Factory Life and Work	Frank H. Hugget.
Mining—Past-into-Present Series	Hugh Bodey.
History Alive: Coal and Mines	Peter Moss.
The Making of the Machine Age	Jacynth Hope-Simpson.
The Early Victorian Woman	Janet Dunbar.
Portrait of Lancashire	Jessica Lofthouse.
Victorian at Home	Susan Lasdun.
Domestic Life in England	Noral Lofts.
Victorian Country Parsons	Donald Jackson.
Occupational Costume in England : the 11C to 1914	Phillis Cunnington and Catherine Lucas.
Handbook of English Costume in the 19C	C. Willet Cunnington & Phillis Cunningham.
Costume and Fashion 1760-1920	Jack Cassin-Scott.

SAPPHIRE

ONE

Lancashire: Spring 1820

From the moment Sapphira Grant opened her eyes she knew it was going to be a bad day at Hickley Vicarage.

The last remnants of sleep were driven away by the heavy footsteps of Zillah Beck, maid-of-all-work, as she thumped her way down to the kitchen. Zillah always stamped when she was out of sorts and that morning the stairs positively quivered under her boots.

Next door, Sapphira's two sisters, Mara aged four and Bethany, six, were wailing like banshees, whilst across the landing the sound of a loud quarrel came from the room shared by her brothers, Ephraim and Shem.

The blankets were thrown back with a groan. It was no good postponing trouble. Sapphira was rising ten and responsible for the ablutions and dressing of Mara and Bethany, charged with the task of getting them to the breakfast table by seven-thirty.

She pulled off her cotton night-shift and washed herself all over, peering into the speckled mirror as she brushed her silky hair. Her sigh was deep, for it was so straight. There wasn't even a trace of a curl as she tied it back with an old ribbon. She

7

was quite unaware of the beauty of her brown eyes, the delicacy of her small nose and perfectly formed lips. All she saw was a thin little girl in a shabby dress who had a dozen jobs to do within the space of half an hour.

St Luke's church and its vicarage were at one end of the village of Hickley, not far from Heald Moor. The parsonage was old and as square as a box, with no architectural features to redeem its plainness. It had six bedrooms, all but one small and stuffy. On the ground floor there was a sitting-room, dining-room, a book-lined study and a large kitchen where the family took their meals when there were no visitors.

As Sapphira herded her sisters downstairs she could hear her father singing hymns as he shaved, Zillah grumbling loudly because the stove wouldn't burn properly, and the continuing argument between her brothers.

The only person who remained unmoved by the noise and wrangling was her mother, Megan. Megan's hair was raven-wing black, like Sapphira's, but drawn up in a large knot on the back of her head. Her complexion was milk-white, her dark eyes luminous, her smile like a benison.

No one was quite sure why Megan Jones, daughter of a well-to-do butcher, had fallen in love with, and married, a dry stick of a curate whose income at the time had been a mere eighty-six pounds a year.

Megan herself wasn't sure why either, as she often told Sapphira in her soft, musical voice which spoke of the Welsh Valleys from whence she had come.

"I knew he was the man for me," she would say, dreaming a bit as she looked back on those days. "Silly I'd have been to turn him down, wouldn't I?"

When the Reverend Decimus Grant finally got the living of Hickley, he received a stipend of two hundred pounds. Even so, the task of running the vicarage and feeding and clothing five children was a Herculean task. There were no luxuries to be had and waste was a mortal sin.

Yet Megan contrived to make life a kind of game for her brood, her lively imagination smoothing the rough corners as

8

she filled her fledglings with the kind of love which money couldn't buy.

When Zillah made black pudding after the November pig killing, stirring in groats and small pieces of fat, Megan brought it to the table, proclaiming it to be *Surprise Noire*. Rice pudding with a crisp crust on top became Princess's Delight, and even the thinnest of broth earned itself the name of *Soup à la Reine*.

When Decimus had kissed Megan fondly on the cheek, he sat down and said grace. He was as thin as a broomstick, with a gaunt, clever face lined with time and worry. To augment his meagre salary he tutored the young sons and daughters of the great houses nearby, for he was a brilliant classical scholar. He not only loved Latin and Greek, he also succeeded in making his pupils enjoy it, too. No one had been more bewildered than he when Megan had agreed to marry him. He worshipped her and never ceased to thank God for her loveliness, her sense of humour, her gentle encouragement and the peace with which she endowed his home.

She worked as hard as he did, but never let that stop her from kissing a grazed knee, or listening to a breathless announcement about the number of frogs just found by the pond in the garden.

She had a gift for sewing and used her needle to good effect. Many people were glad of the gowns, shifts, aprons and caps she produced so swiftly and cheaply. Her one weakness was a pride which wouldn't allow her to admit that she was the seamstress. She told her customers that Zillah did the stitching, daring them to contradict her. Some remained in ignorance of the facts, but most guessed and kept quiet about it. Everyone agreed that she was a reet gradely lass, and humoured her accordingly.

"Zillah, have you remembered that Archdeacon Taylor is coming to tea today"

"Aye. Not likely to forget that, am I? Suppose you'll want a cake baked."

Megan gave Sapphira a quick wink. She and her eldest

daughter were very close and took it in turns to try to sweeten the maid's temper.

"Nice it would be, if we've got all we need for it. Extra work for you, I know, but he's always liked your ale cake."

"So he should, with all them good things in it. Daresay I can scrape together enough flour and fruit."

"I knew you'd manage it somehow." Megan's warmth wrapped itself round Zillah, driving the latter's evil mood away. "Never met a woman before who had such a light hand with a cake as you."

Beck was run off her feet from morning to night, earning a mere pittance for her labours. It never occurred to her to give in her notice. Parson treated her as if she were a fine lady, and mistress would get nowhere without her. She was very protective of Megan, quite happy to enter into the conspiracy concerning the sewing which was done in odd moments and late at night when the children were in bed. It was the kind of pride she understood and anything mistress wanted to do was all right with her.

"I'd like Sapphira to take some things to Mrs Sheldon this afternoon, if that's all right with you, lovey."

Decimus looked up from his lumpy porridge and gave his wife a smile which could still make her heart turn over.

"Of course, my dear. She's getting on very well with her Latin and an hour or two off won't hurt."

Sapphira's spirits lifted at once. There was nothing she liked better than visiting Mrs Petronella Sheldon who lived in the big house on the hill beyond the village. Since the age of six, when she had first started to go to Salter's Lodge, she had wanted to live there herself. She told her family that one day she would do so, ignoring the ribald scoffing of her brothers.

She had inherited her father's intelligence, but a fair share of her mother's optimism as well. Megan was never one to throw cold water on her daughter's dream, seeing nothing foolish in it.

"Why shouldn't she?" she would ask, stroking Sapphira's hair with an affectionate hand. "Pretty enough to marry a prince, she is. Maybe he'll buy the Lodge for her when Mrs Sheldon's dead. Not that I wish her ill, mind, but her time's passing."

"You'll have to wait until after the archdeacon's gone." Decimus sighed as he laid his napkin down. The Venerable Lewin Taylor was a thorn in his side, but he had learned to accept him as the cross he had to bear in life. "He would think it impolite if you weren't here."

"Yes, Papa. I hope he doesn't stay too long."

"So do I," returned her father gloomily. "I always feel so inadequate when he asks how the parish is doing."

Megan's laugh was like velvet on the ear.

"There's silliness for you. He's jealous of you, that's all."

"Jealous of me?" Grant was genuinely amazed. "That can't be so, for he's an important man and very well connected."

"That's why he's got so far. He hasn't a quarter of your brains."

Decimus still looked doubtful.

"I'm very ordinary, you know. If I weren't, I'd have been offered a much better benefice by now, perhaps in London."

"Who wants to live in a dirty town and, as I married you, how can you be ordinary?"

Decimus chuckled, his self-esteem propped up once more by his wife's firmness. He shuddered to think what he would have been like if she hadn't been there to support him. But she always was there, and somehow the dreaded visit no longer seemed to matter.

"It's your birthday next week, Sapphira." Megan turned to other things. "Shall I make you an apron and cap, or maybe we can stretch to a dress."

Sapphira looked at her father thoughtfully. Decimus had given all of his children Biblical names, inscribing them in his faultless handwriting on the flyleaf of the family Bible. Sapphira had never liked the idea of being named after the wife of Ananias and for some time had been waiting to put a proposition to her parents.

"Thank you, Mama, but there's something I'd like more, if

11

Papa doesn't mind. I wouldn't want to hurt him."

Grant looked at his daughter, as beautiful as her mother, and smiled.

"I don't think you could do that, my dear. What is it you want?"

"Well, it's not easy to explain. You may think me conceited or perhaps mad."

"We won't know until you tell us what you're hankering for, will we?" Megan finished her tea, hoping Zillah would make the afternoon brew somewhat stronger. "Come on, pet; out with it."

"I'd like to be called Sapphire instead of Sapphira." Sapphira got the words out quickly, hardly daring to look in her father's direction and trying not to listen to her brothers' hoots of mirth. "It's not that different really, is it? Mrs Sheldon wears a sapphire on a gold chain round her neck. She told me what the stone was; that's how I got the idea. I would truly like that for my present."

"Shem, Ephraim, be quiet." Megan gave them a repressive look. "Always remember to laugh with people, never at them. Mara, wipe your chin and, Bethany, do sit up straight or you'll never get yourself a beau. Before you know it you'll be as drooping as a willow. I think it's a good idea. What do you say, *cariad*?"

Decimus was silent for a moment, wondering if there was some kind of sin lurking in Sapphira's request. Then he decided there wasn't one and nodded.

"Yes, I agree. After all, we didn't give her a choice when she was born. Let that be her gift by all means."

"Then from next Wednesday you will be Sapphire," said Megan, clinching the matter. "And if you boys pester your sister about this I shall find out, be sure of that."

Shem and Ephraim were still grinning, but they were fond of Sapphira whom they thought quite tolerable for a mere girl. Furthermore, they knew better than to cross their mother, easy-going though she was.

Promptly at three-thirty Archdeacon Taylor struggled off his horse, mopping his brow. He was thick-set, with stubby, gaitered legs and purple cheeks, the latter brought about largely by his penchant for port wine.

He hadn't much time for Decimus Grant, whom he considered a nonentity, and refused to let himself dwell on the possibility that he was envious of the man's remarkable scholarship.

He looked around him, taking everything in as if he were making an inventory. There wasn't a decent stick of furniture in the room, but even he had to admit it had an air of cosiness about it.

"Now, you'll have a piece of Zillah's ale cake, won't you?" Megan wore her simple print dress as if it had come from Paris. "She made it especially for you. Disappointed she'd be if you didn't taste it."

Taylor didn't particularly want a slice of stodgy cake made with inferior ingredients. He was used to better fare for, amongst other things, he had the good sense to to marry money. But Mrs Grant was smiling at him and he found himself agreeing that he wouldn't miss it for the world.

He couldn't for the life of him think why this sensuous woman, with a figure which aroused the most unclerical thoughts in him, had married a dried-up failure like Grant. It never ceased to irk him, for it make him aware of what he was missing. Sharing a bed with Megan Grant would be a vastly different matter from lying beside his own wife. The latter might have been rich, but she was also frigid and regarded his tentative advances as coarse and unbecoming to a clergyman.

"Next week, in Sunday School, Sapphira is going to start teaching some of the children from the mines."

Decimus hadn't missed the look which his visitor had bestowed on Megan and had had to find a topic of conversation quickly while he could still keep a straight face.

"Ah, yes." The archdeacon switched his gaze to Sapphira, his lips compressing again. His eldest daughter was plain,

13

spotty and fractious. This child, in her washed-out gingham, was as heart-stopping as her mother. "The more there are to help such unfortunates the better. But be sure to teach them just to read the Bible and nothing more. There is no point in them learning to write or dabble in arithmetic. It would only give them ideas above their station."

Sapphira's eyes met Taylor's and he read the condemnation in them. She was too well-behaved to put her criticism into words, but it was there right enough.

"They'll never do anything but work in the coal mines all their lives," he said sharply. "They're simple souls; it wouldn't do to confuse them with too much knowledge."

"My daughter will follow her father's advice." Megan took Taylor's cup to refill it. "You need have no fear, sir. Sapphira is as capable as you are of judging right from wrong."

"My dear—I don't think—"

Mrs Grant took no notice of her husband's consternation. She had often seen the small children coming up from the pits and had wept for them when she was alone.

"Sad you must be to see mere infants in that condition," she went on smoothly. "Such a kind heart you have. I'm sure you pray nightly that one day they may have just a few of your own blessings."

Lewin's colour grew higher still, but the barb Mrs Grant had just stuck into him had been cleverly fashioned. There was no way in which he could deny the horror of the mines, nor retort that cheap coal required cheap labour.

"Yes, quite." He coughed and looked away. "As you say, her father will see to it that she does what is right. And now I must go—"

"Of course." Megan rose, triumphant because she had won yet another round with the odious archdeacon. "We are grateful to you for sparing time to come and see us. A Godly man, you are, and lucky we are to have you."

When Taylor had gone, muttering something under his breath, the Grants' drawing-room rang with laughter.

"Mama, you were wonderful!" Sapphira clapped her hands.

"He was as red as a turkey-cock."

"And he almost choked on the ale cake," said Shem in delight, for he disliked Lewin just as much as Megan did.

"More's the pity he didn't."

"Don't you think you were—well—perhaps a bit harsh, my love?"

"No, Dessy, and neither do you." Megan was no longer amused. "Don't teach them to write, indeed!"

"We must do as he says."

"Perhaps, but a heart of stone that one has. Thrown down a shaft, he should be, and left there."

Emphraim and Shem agreed loudly, but Decimus looked unhappier still.

"Now who's being un-Christian?"

"I am, and for once I don't care. Boys, finish up that cake or more tantrums there'll be in the kitchen. Come, Sapphira; time it is you were off to Mrs Sheldon's."

She paused in the hall, one finger to her lips. "Don't forget to tell her Zillah made the caps and aprons."

"No, Mama, I always tell her that."

"There's my blossom." Megan gave Sapphira a hug. "It's only a tiny white lie, and it's a position I've got to think about. Wouldn't be proper for people to say your father couldn't keep his family. You understand that, don't you?"

"Oh, yes." Sapphira was very earnest, trying not to giggle. Her mother's attempts to keep up appearances were a family joke, but of the kindest and gentlest sort. "I really, really do, and I love you."

Megan turned on the stairs to look at her daughter.

"I love you, too, sweetling. Now, there's happiness for you, isn't it?"

Sapphira climbed the hill to Salter's Lodge, feeling the familiar excitement grow as she got nearer to the house.

The Lodge, as everyone called it, was a three-storied edifice with low wings flanking it on each side. It had a satisfying symmetry about it which warmed the heart even before one

15

entered the tiled hall.

Mrs Sheldon knew all about Sapphira's love of the place and had allowed her young guest to explore it from end to end. It amused her to see the awe on the face of the Vicar's daughter as the latter stroked the mahogany tables or tip-toed over priceless carpets.

It was Rosena Honey, Mrs Sheldon's personal maid, who opened the door that afternoon. Mrs Sheldon, a widow, lived very quietly and had no use for butlers or footmen. Her cook, Elvira Redding, Honey, and a couple of cleaning women who came in each day were all she needed.

"Mistress says you can wander where you like for ten minutes or so." Honey had grown fond of Sapphira, for the latter's manners were perfect, her smile like the sun breaking through grey clouds. "Then she'll be down to see you."

"Thank you, Honey. I'll be very careful not to disturb anything."

" 'Course you will, and come to the kitchen afore you go. Elvira's got a basket of stuff for Zillah."

It was another white lie, for the sugar, butter, flour, fruit and cold meats were meant for the parson's family. They couldn't be given outright; that would be a sort of charity. They were for Zillah Beck, and that made everything all right.

"How kind you are." Sapphira was as adept at the game as Honey and Elvira. "She'll be so grateful."

With that over, Sapphira went straight to the velvet drawing-room, her favourite place in the Lodge. It was one of the smaller, informal rooms, designed for occasions when no company was expected, but delightful for all that. On the pale green walls were oil-paintings and gilt-framed mirrors. There were Persian rugs and light, delicate pieces of furniture which could be moved easily if the occupant wanted to leave the fire-side and sit by the window.

Sapphira walked over to the desk where Mrs Sheldon did her correspondence, quite lost in the treasure to be found on it. She had inherited her father's love of calligraphy, and thus writing implements and their accessories held a particular

16

fascination for her.

The Sheraton inkstand and paper rack were admired anew, her fingers moving lightly over the sealing wax, candle-stick and Derby incense burner on its stand. There was a leather-covered pocket book, a snuff-box which had belonged to Mrs Sheldon's husband, a silver knife in a case and even a globe which swivelled round to shew the many places in the world which Sapphira hoped to visit one day.

"Ah, my dear, there you are."

Petronella Sheldon was a tiny creature, always exquisitely dressed, with not a hair out of place, and even a touch of rouge on her cheeks for all that she was nearly seventy.

She had never had any children and during the time Sapphira had been visiting Salter's Lodge, she had come to cherish the girl who reminded her of a small madonna.

"Good afternoon, ma'm." Sapphira bobbed politely. "Mother sent these for you, just as you ordered."

"Splendid. Sit down on that stool while I have a look at what you've brought. Honey will be in with the tea in a moment."

Mrs Sheldon's teas aroused almost as much wonder in Sapphira as the articles on her desk. She had never known such wafer-thin bread and butter, nor tasted whole strawberry jam before she had met Petronella. The clotted cream was made in the dairy in one of the Lodge's wings and when that treat was consumed there was always chocolate and sugared biscuits to look forward to. Sapphira had been careful not to partake of Zillah's ale cake, not wanting to spoil her appetite. Sometimes she thought she was guilty of the sin of gluttony, but hoped that God would forgive her lapse and understand that such delicacies really couldn't be refused.

"Your mother's stitches are so fine I can hardly see them. Oh dear! I shouldn't have said that, should I?"

Mrs Sheldon and Sapphira laughed together. Petronella had always known who made the shifts and other things which emerged from the vicarage. She admired Mrs Grant for her industry and unflagging support of her spouse. Now she had given the game away and tried to look contrite.

17

"It's all right." Sapphira helped to fold the aprons up again. "I knew you knew, but mother said I was to tell you Zillah made them, just like last time."

"Well, now you've told me so your duty is done and here's Honey. You must be ready for a bite after trekking up this hill."

"I am hungry." Sapphira admitted it without shame. "But I never mind the walk. Every step I take brings me nearer to your house and when I get to the front door, I'm never sure whether to laugh or cry."

Petronella was aware of Sapphira's longing to live in the Lodge one day, sad because there was no way such a hope could be fulfilled. She would like to have left the place to one who cared so deeply about it, but her nephew had to come first. He seldom visited his aunt, but, as she had once said to Sapphira, blood was thicker than water.

"I expect Henry will sell it," she had said regretfully. "He doesn't care for the country, you see."

"Sell the Lodge!" Sapphira had been horrified, unable to see how anyone could part with something so perfect. "Surely he wouldn't do that?"

"I'm afraid he would—indeed—he will. I wish you could have it, but you do see—"

Sapphira had assured her hostess that she did see. Family always had to come first, but the idea of Henry disposing of such a paradise had depressed her for weeks.

When tea was over, Mrs Sheldon enquired how things were going at the Vicarage and what Sapphira had been doing since they last met. She chuckled at the tale of Archdeacon Taylor's discomfiture, expressed approval that Sapphira was to begin teaching the children from the mines, smiling over the novel birthday present sought from Grant and his wife.

"Well, it's only a few days to go," she said, rising slowly to her feet for her rheumatism was bad that day. "I'll begin to call you Sapphire straight away. I probably won't see you again until after your birthday, so I shall give you my present now."

"Oh, but you don't have to give me anything." Sapphira was stricken with remorse. "I oughtn't to have mentioned next

Wednesday, for it must seem as though I was asking for something. I really didn't mean to."

"You foolish poppet, of course you didn't. Don't you think I know that? In any event, Honey told me two days ago that you'd soon be ten."

Sapphira's unhappiness began to fade. It wasn't really so bad after all.

"How did she know?"

"Zillah told her, I expect. They always have a good gossip on their free afternoons. Now, here is what I want you to have. Take it with my love and use it well."

Sapphira turned pale as Mrs Sheldon put a silver-gilt inkstand into her hands. It was the most splendid thing she had ever seen and at first she couldn't speak.

But Mrs Sheldon understood, touched by the glow in the dark brown eyes. It was such a pity that beauty of that order would go to waste. Sapphira would probably end up as a governess or the wife of an impecunious curate. She should have worn satin and silk, with diamonds round her neck, but of course she never would. Fate was always making a mess of things like that.

She watched her visitor walking away from the house, feeling renewed regret. If only the child had been hers, how different the outcome would be. But there was her sister's son, Henry, to be considered, feckless though he was.

She turned from the window, limping back to her chair. Try as she would, there was nothing she could do to give the girl her heart's desire.

Sapphire Grant would never be mistress of Salter's Lodge.

On the following Wednesday the Earl of Stonehurst arrived at the Vicarage to pay the fees for the tutoring of his son, Ashton Howard, Viscount Rayne, and his daughter Arminta.

He was a tall, well-built man with eyes the colour of chestnuts and thin, well-cut lips. His attire was immaculate, his manner slightly reserved. He hadn't married again after his wife had died giving birth to Minty. He had an heir of whom he was fond and proud, and a girl-child who held his heart firmly in her small white hands, and that was all he wanted.

He had thought it a waste of time for Minty to study Latin and Greek, but she had pleaded to be allowed to go with her brother and, as always, he hadn't been able to refuse her.

The arrival of such an important guest meant that the children were shooed from the study, delighted to have a short break in the bright spring sunshine. They formed themselves into their usual groups; Ephraim and Shem arguing with Sir John Baxter's son as to the best place to fish; the Hon. Michael Streete and Sir William Daneforth discussing Harrow, where they were both to go when they were thirteen, and Rayne, Minty and Sapphire sitting by the rockery, joined after a moment or two by Allene, Lord Quentin Telford's daughter.

"It's your birthday, isn't it?"

Sapphire looked up at Ashton, suddenly shy. At thirteen he was tall, slender and as elegantly clad as his father. His light brown hair had streaks of gold in it, his eyes were hazel, his nose thin and patrician. He might have looked hard or arrogant but for the gentleness of his mouth and the smile which he gave so readily. Sapphire thought him very handsome, feeling honoured because he condescended to speak to her.

"Yes, how did you know?"

"I remembered from last year."

"Ashton's got a good memory." The nine-year-old Minty was a picture in flowered muslin, her fair curls nearer silver than gold. She had hazel eyes like her brother's and the type of beauty which made her appear fragile and vulnerable. "He's brought you a present and so have I."

Sapphire exclaimed over the silk kerchief which Minty had wrapped up so carefully. Like everyone else, she worried about Arminta in case something bad should happen to her. The two girls were fast friends, Sapphire the protector when Ashton wasn't about, Minty the protected.

"Why it's quite wonderful. Dear Minty, how kind you are. I shall keep it always to remind me of you."

"I hope you'll keep this as well, to remind you of me."

Normally, Rayne hadn't got much time for the opposite sex, but Sapphire had earned his approbation because of the way she cared for his sister.

Sapphire accepted the silver pen-knife, made for the cutting of quills, her heart suddenly beating quite fast. She hadn't imagined for a moment the viscount would recall that it was her birthday, let alone go to the trouble of selecting a gift for her.

"It's the best pen-knife I've ever seen," she said in awe. "Thank you, my lord."

"My lord?" he jeered at her, but not unkindly. "I hope you're not going to become prim and proper just because you're ten."

She blushed, knowing he was pulling her leg.

"No, of course not. Thank you, Ashton."

"I'm sorry I haven't brought you anything." Allene was a plump, pretty thing with dimples and fat glossy ringlets. "I didn't know it was your birthday. What did your parents give you?"

Ashton frowned. He had warned Minty not to ask such a question because he knew how poor the parson and his wife were. Minty had understood at once, for she was as sensitive as he. Now Allene had ruined everything by her thoughtlessness.

But Sapphire smiled, unperturbed, telling them of the change in her name.

"I think that's lovely." Minty kissed Sapphire on the cheek. "You're like a jewel anyway, so it's most fitting."

"I like it, too." Allene had seen Rayne's glare but had no idea why he was so cross. "I'd like to alter mine, but Father would never hear of it. I'm called after my grandmother and she's going to leave all she's got to me. She might change her mind if I became Guinevere or Isolde, and she's unbelievably rich. What a bore money is, don't you think?"

Minty thought Allene utterly heartless and slipped her hand into Sapphire's to comfort her, while the viscount said curtly: "No, I don't. For heaven's sake talk about something else."

"But why?" Allene's blue eyes were blanker than ever. "I only said that money—oh! You mean I shouldn't have mentioned it because Sapphire's father hasn't got any?"

Ashton's eyes had grown cold, his mouth a tight line. Sapphire almost shivered, for she had never seen him look like that before.

"Do go away, Allene. You're quite the most stupid girl I've ever met."

When the chastened Allene had departed in tears, Sapphire gave Rayne a quick smile.

"Thank you, but I don't mind, really I don't. It's no secret that we're poor, so there's no sense in pretending otherwise."

"Nor any need to rub it in."

"I'm sure she didn't mean to be unkind."

"Perhaps not, but she should think before she speaks."

Ashton's feathers were still ruffled, but he admired the way Sapphire had taken the knock. He liked courage, whatever form it took, and he gave her an approving nod.

"Mama says money doesn't make people rich."

"Then it doesn't." The motherless Minty liked nothing better than a cuddle on Megan's lap when no one was about. The soft warmth of Mrs Grant's deep bosom, and the lilting voice whispering endearments, were things which even her doting father and brother couldn't give her. "Your mother is always right about everything. What did she say made people wealthy?"

Sapphire knew what Megan meant to Arminta and didn't begrudge her friend a minute of her mother's time. Megan often said that love was like a pool with no bottom. No matter how much one drew out of it there was always plenty more left for others.

"Well, good health; eyes to see with, and ears to hear music. Being able to look at the sky and walk over meadows. To go into the woods and see God's small creatures, like rabbits and mice." Sapphire paused. "I'm not sure I agreed with her about the mice. Still, I knew what she meant. But most of all she said love was what mattered."

"Then we three are vastly rich, aren't we?" Minty stretched out her hand to her brother. "We love one another so we are more fortunate than Croesus."

Ashton felt slightly uncomfortable. Girls were always talking about love and similar nonsense. They never seemed to be interested in important things like hunting and shooting.

His embarrassment ended when Grant rang a bell to summon them back to the study.

"Come on," he said and helped his sister to her feet. "You as well, Sapphire. If you're late on your birthday, you'll be late for the rest of the year."

"Who told you that?" Minty was running to keep up with her brother. "Ashton, you wretch! You're making it up."

"No I'm not." He laughed over his shoulder, striding towards the house. "Mrs Grant told me and, as you've just said yourself, she's never wrong about anything. Hurry, Sapphire, hurry! Who wants to be a slowcoach for the next twelve months?"

TWO

At six o'clock on a fine April evening, Donald Grey was winched up from the depths of Hatley Mine just outside Weir.

He had been far underground since six that morning and the sun, low in the west, made him blink like a mole. His skin was grimed with coal-dust, his breeches soggy with water. Hatley was an old pit, belonging to the Earl of Stonehurst. The seams were no longer rich and some of the former workings were like subterranean pools.

Donald was fourteen, but had started work when he was five. As he trudged home he met a farmer with his wife and children. They gawped at him as if he were a spectacle from a circus. It was always the same. Those who laboured in the dark labyrinth below the bosom of the earth were regarded as a race apart. Small, stunted men, women and children, pallid-skinned under the dirt, too exhausted to hit back at those who averted their eyes in disgust.

But Donald didn't look away. His burning resentment made him out-stare anyone who glanced in his direction. Sometimes he swore at them as he passed them by, hating them for their unspoken judgment.

24

His father, Benjamin, his brothers, Albert and Percy, and his sisters, Olive and Gladys, all worked at Hatley. He never waited for them. They thought him mad because he ran ahead to a spring which came rushing down from the high ground to the east.

Stripped, he knelt on the stony bed of the stream, letting the pure, clear water cleanse him. He rubbed his face and hair until every speck of dust was gone. He even found a sliver of wood, scraping it under his fingernails until they were spotless.

He didn't hurry. There wasn't anything to hurry for. His mother might have stopped drinking long enough to cook any food which was going. Equally, she might be slumped on her mattress by the hearth, snoring off the effects of gin.

She hadn't given him anything for his mid-day meal, letting him go off to slog away for many hours on half a cup of tepid gruel. It had been the same for the rest of the family, but they had accepted the situation passively. Donald hadn't.

It wasn't the first time Beulah Grey had ignored the wants of her children and it wouldn't be the last. He knew that without doubt and made his plans accordingly.

The most vulnerable of the workers were the trappers, some of them as young as four or five. Their job was to open the trap-doors when they heard the corves full of coal trundling towards them. After the carriages had passed, they had to ensure that the doors were tightly closed again. It was vital for the proper ventilation that these infants did their jobs efficiently; the lives of men depended upon it.

Donald himself had started as a trapper. He remembered vividly his first morning, sitting in a small hole hacked out for him in the rock. He had held a string, attached to the door, waiting for the rattle of the approaching corve.

It had been pitch dark and damp. Apart from the women pushing the trucks he hadn't seen a soul from day-break to night-fall. He had thought himself in hell and cried, but when his father came to fetch him he got a cuff round the head for being lily-livered.

He never saw his wages; his father took every penny.

25

Benjamin was as heavy a drinker as his wife and there wasn't much left for the table when they had slaked their thirst.

During the second day of his working life he had encountered an older boy. On that particular occasion Donald had been given a dry crust for his lunch. His fellow-worker had advanced upon him, demanding that the bread be handed over. Donald had fought like a wild thing, but he was no match for his adversary. He had lost the battle and his food, earning another beating from his father for weeping over his defeat.

Now it was he, Donald, who did the stealing. Small girls, crouched in their respective niches, dutifully clinging on to the door strings, were easy prey. They cried, too, as he snatched their oatcakes or thick slices of rye bread away from them, but their dejection left him unmoved. They would have to learn, as he had done, that one had to fight for everything one wanted. People were divided into two classes; the victors and the vanquished. Donald intended to win by whatever means he could.

At last he stood up, tall for his age, with dark curls and amber-coloured eyes which seemed to burn bright yellow when he was enraged. He had often wondered why he didn't look like his brothers and sisters. They had mouse-brown hair, shadows under their eyes, their backs already beginning to bend as a result of the loads they carried. They were plain to the point of ugliness, but he was handsome and knew it.

As he made his way home he was thinking about the future. There wasn't much he could do at present, but in a year or two it would be different. The first priority would be to run away from home. After that he would consider what to do with his life.

He was going to be rich; that was already decided. He would become as well-endowed as the earl who very occasionally came to have a word with the bailiff who managed the pit for him. Donald had studied the cut of Stonehurst's coat, the fine linen shirt, the skin-tight trousers and highly polished boots.

Oddly enough, he hadn't resented the earl for owning a mine which all but destroyed the human beings who laboured in it. His lordship's only concern was the royalties it produced for him. Donald understood that. He proposed to have a colliery in the course of time but, hopefully, one which gave him a better return on his outlay.

Nor would he trouble himself about the people working for him. If they chose to accept their fate, that was up to them. Like Stonehurst, his interest would be what was best and most profitable for himself.

Now that he had become a drawer, dragging the corves to the foot of the shaft, he was growing sturdier. His muscles were developing, his lean body honed into shape by punishing exertion. He didn't mind that either. One needed strength to succeed in life. Eventually, all that he was enduring at present would stand him in good stead.

Each mining village was a self-contained unit, well away from the great houses whose occupants might be offended by the sight of them. The cottages had been put up in a hurry some years before and were already dilapidated. They stood in drab rows, as miserable-looking as those who dwelt in them.

Yet the people sharing common burdens, and thrown together without choice, had become communities. Neighbour helped neighbour, mourning those killed in accidents or dying from fever. They rejoiced at the birth of a child, or when a young couple got married. Mostly they drank and gossiped in the few spare hours they had.

For once Beulah Grey was up and there was broth and boiled potatoes on the table. The others were already eating and no one looked up as Donald sat down and reached for his spoon.

There was seldom any talking at meal times. Everyone was too busy gulping down their food. They hadn't any energy left to chatter; in any event, their father demanded silence while they ate.

Donald was the only one who didn't abide by his father's rules. He had something to say which he'd said many times before. Even the risk of a belting didn't deter him as he raised the subject yet again.

"Pa, have you thought any more about me getting lessons from parson?"

Donald saw the quick look which Benjamin Grey exchanged with his wife, and frowned. He'd seen that sort of glance between them before and hadn't understood it. It wasn't anger or exasperation. It was more like apprehension or even fear.

"Pa, did you hear?"

"Aye, can't but 'elp it, can I? Shut yer mouth or I'll belabour the dayleets out o' you."

"That won't stop me trying again. Why can't I ask Mr Grant to teach me to read and write?"

" 'Cos we've nowt to spare for such nonsense."

Again Benjamin looked furtively at his wife, who had turned quite pale. It was very strange. The only time Donald had seen his parents show emotion of any kind was when he mentioned the subject of education. It was true that there were many other things needed in their household, but Grey wasn't using the family's wages to buy them. He and Beulah were drinking away most of the earnings.

"What if I could get him to teach me free? If I did things for him at the vicarage, maybe he'd agree."

"You've no time for workin' there. If drawin' twelve hours a day don't tire you out, there's plenty to do in this 'ouse."

"You ought to be doing those jobs, Pa."

Albert, Percy, Olive and Gladys turned their heads and gaped at Donald. He had always been the odd one out. He scared them and they made sure they never upset him. They knew he was a bold 'un right enough, but to talk to Pa in such a way was unheard of.

"I'll strap you raw, you whelp! 'Old yer tongue, won't 'ee? Can't a man 'ave a bit o' quiet in 'is own 'ome?"

"Stop moithering yer pa, Donald." Beulah's tone begged him not to press his case. "Like 'e says; man don't want arguments when 'e's done a full day."

The yellowish eyes raked her until she turned crimson. Then Donald said softly: "I do a full day, too, Ma." The threat of a beating had left him unmoved. He'd been whipped so

28

often that it seemed part of the normal scheme of things. Besides, the matter was of crucial importance to him and risks had to be taken. "I earn as well as Pa and the others. But I don't want to drink myself silly when I'm older. I want to learn. Why don't Albert, Percy and the girls want to as well? Everyone ought to be able to write their name and read a book, not just men like the earl and his son."

This time the silence was even longer. Beaulah's mouth was working and her hands unsteady as she got up to side the pots.

"The others don't want to 'cos they've got more sense in their 'eads than you," retorted Grey, avoiding Donald's cool stare. "Shut up, you plaguey boy. Git out o' 'ere afore I skins you alive. You'll be down mines all yer life. What's the use of readin' and writin' to you? Be off wi' you."

Donald was quite ready to go by then. There wasn't anything more to eat and his father wouldn't be budged on the subject of lessons that night.

As he walked away from the village, climbing the steep slope until he could look down on the valley where the earl's house lay, Donald was pensive. There was something going on, he was sure of it, but he couldn't for the life of him imagine what it was. The rejection of his idea had been expected; the reason for the shifty glances and patent fear in his mother remained unresolved.

He stood for a long while gazing at Lindborough Hall. To him, it was all that a house should be. Mellow brick walls; pillars flanking an impressive flight of steps leading up to the front door; perfectly balanced windows, and a landscaped garden with a fountain, a summer house and a folly.

One day, Ashton Howard, a boy near to his own age, would inherit it and with it his father's vast fortune.

In a way he was almost sorry for the viscount because everything would be dropped into his lap. He would miss the tense excitement, the thrilling hazards, and the ultimate satisfaction of becoming a man of substance by virtue of his own wits.

Donald accepted that he himself would never be of the *haut* monde but it didn't bother him. Once he had made his pile there would be any number of people eager and willing to teach him how to dress, which knife and fork to use at table, and how to dance with a beautiful woman. In the end, no one would guess that he had once been a half-starved trapper.

It was then that he made up his mind about the pits he was going to have. Apart from the earl's, there were two within a radius of ten to fifteen miles. The first, Axby, just outside Burnley, belonged to Thomas Clegg. The other, Bluehill, south of the Forest of Trawden, was in the hands of a man called Wilford Broom. The latter was a London merchant and never visited Lancashire. His was by far the best of the mines. Its seams were thicker, its ventilation system more modern, its safety precautions excellent.

"One day I'll have Clegg's pit and Broom's; perhaps Hatley as well." Donald said it aloud, knowing no one was in earshot. "I'll have a house here, as fine as Lindborough Hall. No one will be able to ignore me then; I'll be too powerful for that."

It was common knowledge that the earl wanted to buy Axby and Bluehill and it was a further spur to Donald's ambitions. Like everyone else he had suffered at Hatley. In the course of time his lordship would pay the full price for that.

He stretched his arms above his head, never doubting for a second his ability to achieve his goal. The world was out there, waiting for him to seize it by the throat, but first he needed the assistance of Decimus Grant.

"You'll help me." Donald was smiling as he turned for home again. "They say you've never been known to refuse anyone in need, and I'm in real need now. You won't say no to me, Parson Grant; I'll make sure of that."

A few days later Donald was on his way to his stream when he met Decimus Grant.

He cursed because he hadn't had the chance to wash himself. His present grimed and bedraggled appearance would do nothing to help his cause. On the other hand, he wouldn't have to go to the Vicarage asking to see Grant, a plea which might well be refused.

Fate seemed to be giving him a shove and it was no good just talking about one's aims. Bold action was better than a thousand empty wishes.

As soon as the boy approached him, Decimus felt an odd premonition. At first glance the lad seemed like any other young worker coming off his shift. But a second look showed the finely-cut features and extraordinary eyes which locked with his own.

He listened carefully to what Donald was saying, his doubts increasing. The desire to better oneself was laudable enough, but Grant told himself firmly there was nothing he could do to help. In the end he had to say something and cleared his throat nervously.

"What is your name?"

"Donald Grey, sir, and I wouldn't look like this when I came to you. I always wash before I go home, down there at Lockley Spring."

"I'm sure you do, but there are insuperable difficulties."

"I don't know what that means—in supp—"

"Insuperable; impossible to overcome."

"Nothing is impossible if you want it badly enough."

There was an iron determination in the response, but Grant was equally steadfast in his resolve not to become involved.

"Maybe not, but you couldn't come at the times when I teach. You'd be at work, wouldn't you?"

He saw the small, cold smile and felt his nerves twitch again.

"Don't worry. I wouldn't send your pupils running home because a good-for-nothing came to sit next to them."

Grant was ashamed of his lack of charity and his tremor of fear. Grey was hurting inside because of who he was and what people had done to him. He hoped his own refusal wouldn't add too greatly to the wounds.

"There's nothing I can do, I'm afraid."

"Because I'm not a nobleman's son and can't pay?"

"No, of course not. In God's eyes all men are equal, but—"

"I'd work for you. I'd do anything you told me to. I could

31

chop wood, carry water—anything you wanted."

"You'd only be free in the evenings and on Sunday. How could you undertake such tasks and study at the same time?"

Donald knew then that he was winning. If the Vicar really intended to turn him down he would have walked away by now.

"I'd manage. I'm strong and I don't need much sleep." He could see that Grant was wavering more then ever. A little more pushing, a bit more persuasion, and he'd get what he wanted. "Folk around here say you're a good man. Are you only good to those who already know the alphabet and have money?"

Decimus couldn't look away from the tiger-eyes and was lost. Grey wasn't anything like all the other sad children who lived underground. He was quite different and rather alarming. There was a fierce passion in him; an unswerving resolution which wouldn't be denied. What was more, he, Decimus, was being drawn slowly but inexorably into the web which would fashion Grey's future.

It would mean leaving Megan and the children two or three evenings a week. After doing the rounds of the parish, teaching, writing sermons, visiting the sick and dying, and making sure the registers were kept up to date, Grant was almost as weary as the pit-workers. His few hours of freedom were precious to him, but he found himself saying: "Can you come to the vestry at eight o'clock on Mondays, Wednesdays and Fridays?"

Donald felt relief and triumph flood through him in waves which almost made him tremble. He had done it, and now he had one toe on the first rung of the ladder.

"Yes, I could."

"Would your father object?"

"No." The fib came easily to Donald's lips. "He's out every night anyway, so he wouldn't notice I wasn't there."

"Perhaps not, but you must get his consent."

The second lie was as glib as the first.

"Of course. He'll be glad I'm to better myself."

"Then I'll see you tomorrow." Grant paused. "You do

32

realise how hard it will be for you, don't you? If you've never had any kind of tuition—"

"I haven't."

"Then there'll be a great deal to do. You may find it more taxing than working in the mine."

Again there was a brief, caustic smile.

"Have you ever been down pit, Pastor?"

"No, I haven't. I suppose I ought to have done because those employed there are as much my responsiblity as anyone else, as you've just reminded me. It can't be pleasant."

"It's like being buried, 'cept you don't get the same peace as the dead. You can't rest in that tomb; you have to slave away all the time or the men at the coal face beat you till you vomit. Mines kill, you know. Sometimes they do it quick, like when there's an explosion or flooding. Other times they do it slowly by bending a man's spine bit by bit till it cracks, or filling his lungs with dust until he can't breathe any more."

It was a chilling picture and queer to hear it from the lips of one so young.

"You have a remarkable facility with words and I feel chastened because I live in the daylight."

"Not your fault; just the way things worked out for you." That time Donald's grin was friendly. "You won't be sorry, sir. I'll pay heed to everything you say and work ten times harder than the rest of your pupils. I shan't disappoint you, I swear it."

"No, I don't think you will." Grant couldn't shake off the sense of wariness which had beset him as soon as Grey had walked up to him. It had nothing to do with the boy's lowly birth or his dishevelled appearance. He wasn't sure what it was which made his heart beat faster. He tried to analyse it, but it was too elusive. He told himself he was imagining things and thrust the doubt out of his mind. "Well, goodbye, Donald. We'll see what we can do between us."

But that night as he lay in bed with Megan the qualms returned as he related his encounter with Grey.

"Did I do wrong, my dear? I suppose I should have asked you first since you'll be left alone some evenings."

33

Megan knew Dessy was troubled. She could always tell, for she had been married to him for a long time.

"Such foolishness. What sort of woman would I be if I begrudged him an hour or two of your time! I've cried over those children in the mines often enough. Ill-treated, starving, they are; worked until they can hardly put one foot before the other. Oh, they're dreadful to see. If you can help just one of them it might dry some of my tears."

"I've failed." Grant was full of penitence. "I should have gone down into the pits a long while ago. The boy shewed me that clearly enough. Much as he wanted my aid, he'd no respect for me."

"Then you'll have to earn it, won't you? As for you going into a mine—well! Clumsy, you are, love. You'd bring the roof down on them."

As she laid her head on his shoulder, Decimus said doubtfully: "There was something else."

"I know." Megan was quiet, her banter done. "I saw your face when you came in. What is it?"

"That's the trouble; I'm not sure." Grant closed his eyes, fishing for a sensible explanation which wouldn't come. "He isn't like anyone I've met before. I sensed—"

"Ambition?"

"That, certainly, but I could deal with his high aspirations."

"Then what?"

Megan felt a shudder run through Dessy's spare frame.

"I think it was evil, or something very like it."

Megan was startled but she shewed no sign of it. Dessy hadn't finished yet. He was till trying to get things straight in his mind.

"Evil? There's a strong word for you."

"Yes, perhaps too strong. It was a kind of ruthlessness, the sort which would let nothing stand in its way, no matter the cost."

"Not like you to reject a child."

"I haven't rejected him. I'm going to do what he—what he asked of me."

34

"Asked? What were you going to say? You hesitated."

His sigh was deep and he was very glad of the warmth of Megan's body close to his. There was solace and safety in her arms and he began to unwind.

"I was going to say demanded, and he isn't a child. I'm an idiot, aren't I? Why do you love me?"

"Now there's a question, isn't it?" Megan was trying to throw off her own disquiet. She wasn't a Celt for nothing and her husband's worry had crept into her own heart. Dessy had never spoken in such a way before. There had to be something very strange about Donald Grey who, for all his youth, wasn't a child. She refused to give in to her weakness. The pit lad may have wanted help, but so did her husband. "Fancied you the moment I set eyes on you. Must be your strapping great body, or all those sovereigns you keep hidden under the mattress."

"You could have done so much better for yourself."

Her hand began to stroke his chest, fingers light as feathers, arousing him as she gave a seductive laugh.

"No I couldn't, and if you believe that it is an idiot you are. Come here, my dear sweet silly one. Isn't it about time you gave me a proper kiss?"

On the following Sunday, Sapphire began her Bible class. An old store next to the vestry had been cleared and scrubbed, the benches already there given a good rubbing by Zillah.

When Grant had first arrived at Hickley hardly anyone attended Sunday School. The overworked children were too tired to drag themselves to church, their parents wholly uninterested in something which brought in no money.

Predictably, it was Megan who solved the problem of Decimus's failure to lure the young towards the path of righteousness. One Saturday she and Zillah baked some extra loaves, cutting them into thick slices on the following morning and spreading them with a mite of butter and some plum jam made by Mrs Sheldon's cook. They had put the plates on a pew beside the font, Zillah making it her business to see that word of their activities reached the village. That afternoon, Grant was astounded to find two dozen children waiting for him, a number which had gradually increased as the months went by.

Sapphire had her own rickety table with three plates piled high with wedges of fresh bread and jam, but she was made of sterner stuff than her father.

As her pupils, aged four to eight, rushed into the improvised classroom she ordered them out again to wash their hands and faces at the pump. Some looked at her rebelliously, but she was adamant.

"No washing, no food," she said firmly. "Cleanliness is next to Godliness. Besides, you'll eat as much dirt as bread as you are now."

She had intended to make them wait until after the lesson, but their pathetic hunger and wan faces had touched her soft heart. She watched them wolf down their treat, saddened because there was so little she could do for them. Archdeacon Taylor had even forbidden her to teach them to write or do sums to better themselves. He was quite content to consign them to their present unhappy lot for the rest of their days.

The thought of the archdeacon, probably stuffed with prime roast beef, vegetables, and a fruit pie made her blood boil. She would have to obey his dictum or her father would get into trouble. It was so unfair, but at ten it was hard to right such wrongs.

Most of the children dozed through her painstaking explanation of the alphabet. It was disheartening, but Sapphire couldn't blame them. Twelve or more hours a day for six days a week, combined with full bellies, made eyelids droop and limbs slacken. One girl even snored slightly as her head rested against the wall.

When it was time to go, Sapphire went up to her and smiled.

"What is your name?"

"Essie, Miss; Essie Gosling."

Sapphire looked at her thoughtfully. She was small and wiry with straggly hair, a snub nose, a mouth too big for her face and a game leg. But there were compensations, too. Nature had given Essie a pair of eyes like pale emeralds and a smile which

36

made a lump rise in Sapphire's throat.

"Tell me about yourself. How old are you?"

"Eight, Miss."

"Does your family live in the village?"

The smile faded into melancholy.

"What's left of it. Pa and me four brothers were killed three years since. There's only me, me sister Lucy, and Ma left and Ma's crippled."

"You mean like—"

Sapphire bit off the question, but Essie didn't mind. She was used to taking blows, physical and otherwise.

"No, she's worse'un me. Got 'er legs broke when part of roof fell in. They pulled 'er out awkward like, so she can't walk no more."

"I'm terribly sorry." Sapphire was mortified. "I didn't mean to upset you. I ought to mind my own business."

The lovely smile washed Sapphire's contrition away.

"I don't mind. Quite nice to talk to someone about it now and then. Lucy don't understand and Ma's in too much pain. It ain't easy, won't say it is. But me and Lucy work as trappers and we get by most of the time. Overseer said I might be a drawer in a month or two. Most girls of my age are drawers already, but there's me leg, you see. Makes me slow."

"How did you hurt it?"

"Door slammed on it. It were when I were five, so I'm used to it. Some o' the boys calls me old lamey, but I don't take no notice of 'em."

"That's very unkind of them."

"Most folks are unkind, Miss."

Essie wasn't whining; it was a statement of the human condition as she saw it.

"Some people are, I know, Sapphire said gently, "but not all of them. I hope you'll find that out one day. Do you want to learn to read the Bible?"

"Not much."

"Then why did you come today?"

" 'Cos of the bread and jam. I allus come on a Sunday for

37

that but usually your pa takes the class."

"Yes, it's my first day. Did you sleep through his lessons, too?"

Essie had the grace to blush.

"Didn't think you'd noticed. Yes, I used to drop off when 'e were talkin'. 'E's got such a soothin' voice and I'm that tired."

"I understand, I really do. But try to stay awake in future. If you can read, it will open new worlds for you. There are so many wonderful books for you to enjoy."

"I'll try. Ma said I ought to get what learnin' I can."

"She's right. Forgive me for asking this, but is that the only dress you have?"

Essie glanced down at the torn rag she was wearing. It hadn't seen water for weeks, except the muddy pools in the mines. It had been old when it was first given to her. It had belonged to Mrs Weeks' daughter, Mabel, and she'd had her penny-worth out of it before passing it on.

"Yes, ain't got no money to buy more, what with ma laid up all the time."

"No, I see that. Would you be offended if I asked my mother whether you could have one I've outgrown? I hope you don't think that sounds like charity."

"I'd be reet grateful and charity don't worry me. I've learned to take what I can get. You 'ave to, if you want to live."

Megan looked down at the wide green eyes as she listened to Sapphire's explanation.

"Good gracious, what troubles you've had. Are you still hungry?"

" 'Fraid so. I 'ad a bit o' bread, but that soon went down. We don't 'ave much at 'ome, you see."

Zillah was hovering, her eyes moist. She'd seen dozens of mine children before, but there was something about this scrap of a human being which touched her very vitals.

"Reckon I could find a bite of summat, ma'm, if it's all right with you."

"Of course it is. Wrap up a couple of loaves for Essie to take with her and fill that big stone jar with broth. Ephraim or Shem can help to carry it. Now, food first, then a good wash down in the tin bath. After that we'll see what we can find for you to wear."

"And Lucy, Mama? She's four."

"There's good fortune for you, Essie. Mara, my youngest, is the same age. I've just washed a dress of hers which she can spare."

"I suppose there's no hope—"

Megan smiled at Sapphire, reading her daughter's thoughts with ease.

"Got a length of print only the other day to make myself a new gown. Mrs Gosling can have my green cotton and welcome she is to it."

For the first time Essie's stalwart spirit deserted her and tears began to trickle down her cheeks.

"Lovey, what is it?"

Essie looked up at the parson's wife. Until then she had only seen Mrs Grant from a distance, but close to she was like a queen. She wanted to bury her head against Megan and let loose all the sorrows nursed inside herself for so long. Megan sensed it and pulled her nearer.

"There's a silly one. You sit here with me for a bit while Zillah and Sapphire get things ready."

"I didn't mean to—"

"Of course you didn't. Such a brave wee thing, you are." Megan sank into her rocking-chair and drew Essie on to her lap.

"Now, that's better, wouldn't you say?"

"I'll make you all dirty, like me."

Megan closed her eyes, holding the child against her.

"No, you won't. Just you let go for once. God doesn't expect courage all the time; too sensible for that, He is. There, there, you cry away while I have a word with Him about you and your ma."

For a moment Essie raised her head.

"And Lucy?"

"Of course; Lucy too."

39

"Will He listen?"

Megan kissed Essie on the forehead, her arm tightening round the skinny body pressed close to her own.

"Oh, yes, *cariad*," she said softly, "He'll listen; He always does. There's a blessing for us all, isn't it?"

THREE

Four years later Donald knelt beside Beulah Grey's mattress watching her loosen her hold on life.

Benjamin Grey had been killed a few months before and when Beulah caught a chill she hadn't put up a fight for survival. When she knew the end was near she sent the others outside. There was something she had to say to Donald and she knew she hadn't got much longer to go.

At eighteen Donald was tall and straight despite the rigours of the mine. When he wasn't working or studying he ran for miles to ensure that his body would remain healthy. He had learned a great deal since he had first gone to St Luke's vestry that spring evening. His mind was quick and he had an insatiable appetite for knowledge which had amazed Decimus Grant.

Grant had lent Donald many books to read and at night the latter would creep out of the cottage and into the shed, armed with stubs of candles which he had purloined earlier in the day. By their flickering light he had devoured everything, scribbling a note of any questions he wanted to ask the Vicar at their next meeting. His family remained in ignorance of his scholarship and none of the men at the coal face ever discovered what happened to their candles.

"Donald—summat I must tell 'e."

Donald was no fonder of Beulah than he had been years before, but he recognised the oncoming of death and respected it.

"No need to worry yourself, Ma."

"Must—must. Couldn't go wi'out puttin' things reet."

"What things?"

" 'Bout the night 'ee were born."

Donald frowned. His parents had never mentioned anything unusual about his birth. He assumed he had come into a world of dirt and pain like Albert, Percy and his sisters.

"I don't understand. What was special about that night?"

Beulah's eyes were bright with fever, her breath tearing at her throat, but she hung on. She had always had an unease in her about Donald, but Benjamin had forbidden her to mention the secret. Now Benjamin wasn't there and her conscience had to be freed before she joined him.

"You—you're not my son—nor Benjamin's neither."

Donald kept very still, not wanting to waste the dying woman's time with unnecesssry questions. As he waited for her to continue his mind slipped back to those occasions when he had seen her full of fear, exchanging inexplicable looks with Grey.

"Yes?" he said quietly. "Go on, if you can."

"Have—have to go on. You were t'Earl of Stonehurst's bastard. 'E wanted to be rid of 'e afore 'is wife found out what 'e'd been up to."

"Why you?"

" 'Cos Benjamin 'ad been caught stealing. 'Is lordship said 'e'd 'and 'im over to the authorities unless we agreed. Gave us a tidy bit o' money and said we were to bring you up as our own. Couldn't say no; it 'ud 'ave meant prison or worse for Benjamin and I'd 'ave lost me job in t'mine."

Donald could feel himself grow burning hot with the stifling rage in him. He was Stonehurst's son and he'd been left to rot

42

in a miner's hovel. He thought about Ashton Howard, grinding his teeth. He should have taken his place beside Ashton. He could never had inherited the title, but the earl had had no right to throw him aside like an unwanted mongrel.

"You should have told me," he said finally. "I had a right to know."

"Aye, that you did, but the earl told us to keep our mouths shut. He'd not have admitted you were, is, even if—even if we'd spoken up. Who'd—who'd have believed the likes of us against his lordship? Anyways, yer pa—that is—Benjamin had spent all o' the money."

"Ma—I mean—"

A faint smile touched the bloodless lips as Beulah looked at Donald.

"Call me that till I go. After that—don't matter."

"All right. Who was my real mother, do you know?"

"Mm. She were a pretty wench with eyes the colour o' yours. 'Ad dark curls like 'ee. Name of Flora Brown."

"Where did the earl meet her?"

"She worked for 'im for a while. Donald, give us a drop o' water, there's a boy. Me throat's that dry."

Carefully Donald raised Beulah, holding the chipped cup to her lips. When she sank back with a murmur of thanks he said: "What happened then?"

"After he knew she were carryin' 'e packed 'er off. She lodged with Mrs Bowker until you came."

"Where did she go? Why didn't she keep me?"

Beulah made one last effort.

"She died givin' birth to you. Never even saw you, not once."

The anger grew fiercer and Donald's mouth was ugly with bitter resentment.

"His lordship's got a lot to answer for. It was because of him that my mother died. His fault that I've lived like a serf for all this time. I'll make him suffer though, never fear. I've kept a secret from you, too, Ma. I've been taking those lessons from parson I was always on about when I was younger. Four years

43

or more Mr Grant has been teaching me. He says I've got an outstanding mind. What do you think about that? I reckoned it was just a quirk of Nature when he said it. Me, a miner's son, clever enough to go to university, if we'd the money. But it wasn't a quirk, was it? I've got Stonehurst's blood in my veins and I've inherited his intelligence, if nothing else. Christ! How could he have done such a thing to me? I'll force him to acknowledge me in the end. I'll go to London and earn some money. No one gets anywhere without that, and now I'm able to make all I'll need. I've got the knowledge and a better reason than ever to become a rich man. When I'm ready I'll come back here, only no one will recognise me. I'll be in fine clothes, living in a big mansion, with fancy manners and fine airs. No, Stonehurst will never guess and I'll choose my own time to tell him who I am. Ma, are you listening?"

For a few minutes Donald stared down at the dead woman beside him. He felt no regret at her passing, for she had never meant anything to him. Furthermore, she had let him slave in the mines because she was afraid to cross her master. Still, in the end she had confessed and in any event all his venom was reserved for his natural father.

He rose and went to the shelf where an old tin contained what money the family possessed. It wasn't much, but Donald took it all, forcing Beulah's wedding ring from her left hand.

Luckily there was no one outside when he opened the door. Those he had believed to be his brothers and sisters were nowhere to be seen and he bared his teeth. No wonder he didn't look like they did. They were the offspring of Benjamin and Beulah Grey; he was the son of an earl.

It was Sunday morning, so Grant and his family were in church along with their maid. He had no difficulty in getting into the parsonage and finding the room occupied by Ephraim and Shem. Ephraim was about his age and size and he took what clothes he could find, together with a new pair of boots which Ephraim had been given for his birthday.

He guessed the parson's wife would keep something tucked away, just as Beulah had done. He searched the kitchen for a while, triumphant when he found two guineas in a tea-pot with no spout. But he wasn't finished yet.

He crept into the vestry, hearing the congregation singing to a God in whom he had no faith. Not for a second did he consider the debt he owed to Decimus Grant for all those hours of patient tutoring. He broke open the poor box and rifled a drawer which contained money collected for repairs to the church roof.

He paused for a second at the stool where he had sat so often. It was old and uncomfortable, but he had never noticed that. He had been too busy listening to Grant or poring over his books. Above the table on which he had written essays, studied Latin and French, or worked out mathematical problems, there was a stone plaque. It was very old and he had stared at it many times whilst he was waiting for answers to come to him. It was in memory of Sir Geoffrey FitzMaurice of Lyndon Hall, who had died in 1483. The centuries had worn Sir Geoffrey's profile away, but his name stood out clearly enough and Donald needed a new name.

Donald Grey was as dead as Beulah and had to be done away with for ever.

"Lyndon FitzMaurice." He said it under his breath, his imagination fired by its aristocratic ring. "That's who I'll be from this moment on. When I return, no one will suspect I've borrowed your name and that of your home. Who looks at relics like you, my lord?"

Down at Lockley Spring he tore off his stained garments, washed himself thoroughly and donned Ephraim's clothing. He buried his own rags and put the spare shirt and trousers in a bag he had found in the parsonage kitchen.

As he ran away from Hickley no shred of his corrosive fury had abated. It was not only the earl who would be crucified in the course of time, but the viscount and his sister as well. Lyndon, for he had lost no time in thinking of himself as such, doubted whether Ashton or Arminta knew anything about their illegitimate half-brother. The earl would hardly have boasted of such a matter to his pampered brats. But their

45

ingorance wouldn't save them from retribution. They were part of the family which had spurned him and would have to pay the price for that along with their father.

When he was far enough away from the village and Lindborough Hall for safety, he turned back to look over his shoulder.

"Good riddance to you all," he shouted at the top of his voice. "But you haven't seen the last of me. And you, my Lord Stonehurst, enjoy what life you've got left to you, for when I come again it will be to destroy you. Do you hear me? In the end I'll kill you, damn you. I'll kill you!"

"He was so intelligent—such a fine mind. I never expected to find one so clever amongst the villagers." Decimus was stricken when the news came of Donald's flight. He hadn't wanted to believe the boy had stolen from the Vicarage and the church, but in the end he had to accept it. For all his efficiency, Donald had dropped the knife he had used to prise open the poor box and Grant had seen him use it many times to sharpen quills. "Yet I sensed from the beginning that he was amoral."

"I remember." Megan was as upset as her husband. Decimus had been so proud of his protégé. Now the ingrate had thrown his mentor's kindness in his face. "You said he was ruthless and I thought you fanciful. I should have paid more heed to you, for it's wiser than me you are."

"I'm so sorry, Papa." Sapphire sat on a stool by her father's side holding his hand to comfort him. "He's thoroughly wicked."

Grant smiled sadly.

"No, my dear, not really. Wicked people are those who know right from wrong but sin anyway. In many things, Donald really couldn't distinguish one from the other. As your mother says, I did have a feeling about him when we first met and later I knew I wasn't mistaken. So many small things, not significant in themselves, but together the picture was clear enough for those with eyes to see. I deliberately blinded myself to his faults. I was filled with terrible pride because I had found a poor youth with a brain superior to my own. I wanted nothing to spoil my creation of a scholar and so I ignored his soul, may God forgive me."

"I'm sure He will, lovey. Don't blame yourself so. Donald deceived you."

Decimus shook his head.

"No, I deceived myself and that's much worse."

When her father had gone to the church to pray for absolution and Megan had bustled back to the kitchen, Sapphire continued to sit on her stool, her own conscience far from clear.

At fourteen she had grown to willowy slenderness, still unaware of her own loveliness. All she knew was that she was being underhanded in the way she had been conducting her Sunday School classes for the past year.

Her enthusiasm had been strong enough to capture the attention of her pupils and most had become quite proficient at reading the scriptures. On her thirteenth birthday she had decided to teach the miner's children to write and to introduce them to the solving of simple sums.

There were no slates to be had, nor had she dared to ask her father for any. He would have stopped her scheme at once, fearful of what Archdeacon Taylor would say. She had started to do some sewing, like Megan, making a little money for herself. She used it to buy paper and quills, but there was never enough to go round.

Three children had to share half a sheet of paper and a quill, taking it in turns to sit by the door, keeping a weather eye out for the approach of the Vicar.

She kept thrusting her sinfulness away as she exhorted the class to work hard at their letters. "Knowledge is power," she would say, wondering what difference knowledge would really make to her small, down-trodden flock.

She had had no idea that her father had been teaching Donald Grey. It was something he had kept to himself until the wretch had robbed him and disappeared. She tried to convince herself that her secret was no worse than her father's had been, but she knew it was. One day Archdeacon Taylor would pay a surprise visit to St Luke's and catch her in the act.

She didn't particularly care what the archdeacon said to her. As his girth had grown, so had her scorn of him. It was her father who would bear the brunt of his superior's wrath, and he had enough troubles as it was without her adding to them.

At last she rose, her sigh deep. If her repentance had been genuine, like her father's, she would be making plans to abandon the quills and ink and scraps of paper. As it was, her determination to help the children was stronger than ever. Whatever lesson there was to be learned from Donald Grey, Essie and the others were going to get their chance.

"So fiddlesticks to you, Mr Archdeacon," she said defiantly, and took herself off to the kitchen to help with the baking.

"What a rascal," said Mrs Sheldon indignantly when Sapphire had related Grey's wrong-doings. "How hurt your poor father must be."

"He is, although he blames himself. He says he neglected Donald's soul."

"I doubt if the rogue has one. Has this given you second thoughts about what you're doing?"

Petronella knew all about Sapphire's classes and what went on in them. She admired the girl for trying to help the children of the poor, but privately she considered Sapphire's efforts weren't going to be of much use in the long run.

She had noticed once or twice, when Sapphire had spoken of her Sunday afternoons, that the girl's eyes were troubled. That day, Sapphire's unease was too obvious to ignore.

"It worries you that your father doesn't know what you're doing, doesn't it?"

Sapphire accepted a cup of tea, the rose-painted china so thin one could almost see through it.

"Yes, it does. I've always hated that part of it and now, after what Donald Grey did, I feel worse than ever."

"Why don't you make a clean breast of it? I'm sure your father would understand."

48

"Yes, he would, but he wouldn't let me go on. He'd make me stop because of Archdeacon Taylor."

"A very stupid, self-centred man."

"Yes, he is, and a snob as well, but we can't escape from him. Only yesterday he called and talked about the Sunday School. It was the same as always. The children must learn to believe in God, but not in themselves. They will hew coal all their lives, so they may never have the satisfaction of reading Shakespeare or Milton, or anything else come to that."

"I doubt if he reads Milton himself. He hasn't got the brains."

"No, but he could make things very difficult for Papa if he found about about the lessons. Still, I won't be able to go on much longer anyway."

"Why not?"

"I'm running out of paper and quills and I don't make enough money with my sewing to buy any more for quite a while. I'm very economical, but there are more children coming nowadays. It's a pity, but perhaps that's the way God is punishing me."

Petronella studied the sad, exquisite face and wished Sapphire was her daughter. It was a longing which had assailed her many times, but never more strongly than at that moment. In the end she said casually: "I don't think the Almighty would punish you for trying to help others."

"I think he might. That's why He won't let me earn enough to get more materials."

"You're wrong. He's going to give you what you need."

Sapphire looked up quickly.

"Is He? How?"

Petronella gave a conspiratorial wink.

"I have enough paper to last you for five years, and more quills than I can count. I don't write many letters nowadays and at my age my conscience is very flexible."

"You mean it? You truly mean it?"

"Yes, my dear, I mean it."

"But that's wonderful! Perhaps I'd better not take all of the paper at once, otherwise someone might discover my hoard."

"Very sensible. If you're going to be a plotter, be a good one."

Sapphire's happiness melted away.

"Yes, you're right. I am still plotting, aren't I? Your generosity doesn't alter my sin."

"Which is stronger in you?" Mrs Sheldon said quietly, "your own transgression or your wish to assist those less fortunate than yourself?"

Sapphire didn't need time to weigh her answer in the balance.

"My wish to give those children some hope."

"Then don't stop. You'll have to pay for your decision with a restless night or two but you're strong enough to endure those. Now, if you've finished your tea, would you like to look around the house again? I shall go up and have a nap, but you take your time. You never seem to tire of Salter's Lodge."

"I'd love to walk about a bit, if I may. And, no, I shall never tire of it. It gives me a sense of peace, because everything in it knows its right place."

"Yes, Honey's a tidy woman."

"I didn't really mean that sort of right place. It's hard to explain, but each piece of furniture seems to have been made especially for the room it's in and the spot where it's standing. The ornaments and pictures couldn't exist anywhere else, because they belong exactly where they are."

"I suppose that's because they've been there for a long time."

"And they'll still be there in a hundred years."

Sorrow crept over Mrs Sheldon again as she got up, leaning on her stick.

"I doubt that."

Sapphire came back to earth with a bump.

"No, of course not; I forgot. Your nephew will sell it, won't he?"

"I fear so. My dear, if only—"

Quickly Sapphire moved forward and planted a light kiss on

50

Mrs Sheldon's cheek.

"I know, you don't have to say it, or be sad about it. Whatever happens in the future, no one can take my memories of it away. Memories do matter, don't they?"

"Yes." Petronella's mind had winged back to the days when her husband, Stephen, had brought her to the Lodge as a young bride. He had been strong and handsome, she very much in love. He had died old and sick, but she never thought of him that way now. The man who walked beside her every day, and shared her bed at night, was an Adonis of twenty-four. "Yes, you're right. In fact, sometimes I think memories are the most important things we mortals possess. Be sure to keep yours, child, for when you're at your life's end, as I am, they'll probably be all you'll have left."

After Mrs Sheldon had gone, Sapphire went into the orangery. She wasn't in the least acquisitive, and was generous to a fault, but she had one more prayer to say before she left for home.

"I know it would take a miracle, Lord, but do you think Mrs Sheldon could live a few years more until I'm grown up? Then, perhaps, I might marry a rich man and he'd buy the Lodge from Henry. I realise I'm greedy to ask for so much, and perhaps you think I'm being idolatrous into the bargain, but please, please do consider it. Oh, I do so want to be mistress of Salter's Lodge one day."

On her way back to the Vicarage Sapphire met Viscount Rayne, home for a while before going up to Oxford.

Sapphire hadn't seen much of him since he went away to school, but she never forgot him. He was the god-like creature to be adored from afar, who had remembered her tenth birthday.

Ashton waved as he saw Sapphire, but as she got nearer he felt an odd tremor run through him. He had always thought the Vicar's eldest daughter a pretty girl, but now she was breathtaking. A fourteen-year-old about to step into woman-hood. Her dark hair streamed down her back, her slim body moved lightly over the grass with consummate grace. When he looked into her eyes he knew at once that something was happening to him and was afraid of the consequences.

He recognised the admiration in her, but that was the same old hero-worship she'd always had for him. It wasn't what he wanted from her, but perhaps it was just as well that she was too immature to realise it.

Already his father was talking about a betrothal between himself and Allene Telford. He had never liked Allene very much, but the earl had made plain the fact that one wasn't expected to be in love with one's wife. It was a good match which counted; one looked elsewhere for pleasure.

When they had exchanged greetings, Sapphire colouring at Ashton's warm smile, he took her parcel from her.

"What are you carrying so close to your heart? Diamonds? No, it's too heavy for that? A golden urn?"

She didn't mind him teasing her; he had always done that. It was so good to be with him again and she had forgotten just how handsome he was.

"No, it's more valuable than that."

"More valuable than diamonds and gold? I give up?"

"It's paper and some quills."

"Good heavens, you're not becoming a blue-stocking, are you? Of course, you always were good at Greek and Latin. We were all envious of you because you found your exercises so easy."

Sapphire's blush deepened.

"Were you? I didn't know that. I don't think I was particularly clever. It was just that father started to teach me when I was very young."

"He couldn't have done that if you were a dullard. What's the paper for? Are you going to write a book, like Jane Austen?"

She laughed, her nervousness gone. In spite of his sophisticated appearance he was still the same, easy companion of childhood.

"Gracious, no! I should have no notion how to draw my characters nor think of a plot to hold the attention of my readers. No, it's for my Sunday School classes."

"So you teach now, do you? Tell me about it."

Sapphire did so with enthusiasm, until she confessed her subterfuge.

"But it's so important, don't you think?"

Rayne was frowning. He had never had any dealings with the miners' children and wasn't even sure what they looked like. His father had forbidden him to go near Hatley and certainly none of the young workers had come within miles of Lindborough Hall.

"Ashton, don't you think so?"

He came out of his reverie as Sapphire repeated her question, gazing into eyes which glowed with the fervour of her cause.

"I'm not sure."

"You can't be serious! You couldn't really begrudge them a smattering of knowledge. They've got so little chance in life."

"I know, that's why I'm not sure that what you're doing is wise."

"You sound like Archdeacon Taylor."

"Oh dear, do I?"

"Exactly. He says that those who will always have to work underground need only learn to read the Bible. He would rob them of the opportunity of better things. He's a pompous bigot."

"So he may be, but have you ever stopped to consider whether he may be right as well?"

"No, I haven't. How can preventing the young from having some education be right?"

"Because it might awaken in some of them hopes which can never be fulfilled. They would become restless."

"So they should." Sapphire's indignation was growing. "I thought that you, of all people, would approve."

"And I've disappointed you. I'm sorry."

They had stopped for a moment, the viscount too honest to win Sapphire's approval with lies. He wanted to be done with the subject anyway, and talk of other things, but she looked as if she were about to strike him dead on the spot.

He said softly: "You are very beautiful, did you know that?"

His words took Sapphire completely by surprise and her anger fled as quickly as it had come.

"No—no, I didn't."

"Well, you are. You should be doing other things with your time, not wasting it on children who aren't worth—"

He saw her lips tighten.

"All right, all right," he said hastily, "I withdraw that. Don't let's quarrel. We haven't got much time together. Pax?"

His smile was irresistible and Sapphire was only too well aware how short their meeting would be.

"Pax."

"I could always win you round."

"Ashton! You're a beast."

"That's what Minty calls me when she's losing an argument. She tells me that you see her quite often."

"Yes, we meet at church and sometimes when she is out riding with her companion. She is so lovely."

"Yes, she is. You'll go on looking after her while I'm at Oxford, won't you?"

Sapphire saw nothing odd in the request. Arminta had her father, a chaperon, a maid, and a large staff of servants to tend her, but Sapphire knew what Aston meant.

"Of course; you know I will."

He was sober now, his laughter gone.

"Ever since we were small children I felt that Minty was different from other people. It's as if she's walking towards some sort of danger and I know I won't be able to help her when the time comes."

Sapphire didn't want to add to Ashton's anxiety, but her own thoughts had always run on the same lines. Minty was sweet and gentle and vulnerable and had to be watched over.

"Between us we'll manage," she said finally. "I promise I'll do my best."

He relaxed, his fear gone for a while.

"Thank you; that makes my mind easier."

There was silence between them as they stood close together, the wind ruffling Ashton's hair and whipping Sapphire's skirts about her ankles. When he laid his hand on her cheek Sapphire was bewildered by the stab of pain inside her. They had always been friends, but he had never touched her before. She hadn't expected him to do so then, and she wasn't sure that she liked the change in their relationship, slight though it was.

Rayne walked away quickly, not wholly certain of his feelings either. He tried to pretend that his gesture was merely one of gratitude because of Sapphire's promise, but he knew he was fooling himself.

He had wanted to put his arms round her and steal a kiss, and he swore as he turned in the direction of Lindborough Hall. She was only fourteen, not much older than the children she taught so devotedly each Sunday. By the time she really was a woman, he would be engaged to Allene and that would be that. Whatever emotions Grant's daughter aroused in him they had to be dowsed once and for all. There was about as much hope for him and Sapphire as for the trappers in the mines. His life was mapped out in one direction, hers in another.

At all costs he mustn't fall in love with her, for that would be madness. He had to forget all about the unfamiliar desires which were so new to him, and which he really didn't understand. The dark-haired girl, with eyes which made him giddy when he looked into them, must be pushed back into the past from whence she came. She had no place in his future and never could have. However much he regretted it one thing was clear. The enchanting Sapphire Grant would never belong to him.

FOUR

Lyndon FitzMaurice arrived in London on a wet Monday afternoon. The journey on top of the coach had been acutely uncomfortable, but he had no intention of paying extra for the privilege of travelling inside. Every penny mattered until he could find work, and he had managed without food for many hours.

He wandered through the City, awed by its dignity and splendour. Even the pouring rain couldn't dim its importance and he knew then that he had made the right choice. It was in the capital where he would make the fortune for which he craved. The opportunities were all around him, waiting for him to take them.

His head was so full of future plans that he didn't stop to consider where he would sleep that night. He left that problem for a later hour when his dreaming was over.

After a while the pangs of hunger grew too biting to ignore and he paused to count the money in his pocket. It would last him for a few days, if he were careful. He was just wondering whether the City contained such dull things as shops where one could buy bread and cheese, when he heard a man cry out.

Afterwards, Lyndon was never sure why he answered the call for help. Assisting others didn't interest him; every man had to look out for himself. But it was as if Fate were pushing him again, making him run swiftly over the slippery pavement to where two ruffians were attacking a man on the ground.

Whatever other qualities Lyndon lacked, he had plenty of courage. He also had much experience of dirty fighting, for in the mines one had to hit out hard and fast or end up bruised and bloodied.

The two villains made off in a hurry, realizing they had met their match, and Lyndon bent to help the victim to his feet. He was about fifty years of age, very well-dressed, with an aura of affluence about him.

"Thank you, m'boy. That was a timely intervention. Might have lost more than my purse if you hadn't come along."

"You're not hurt, sir?" Lyndon knew at once the role he had to play. Courteous deference, apparent respect, but enough fire in him to interest the man he had rescued. "Have you lost much?"

"Nothing. They didn't have time to get their hands into my pockets. As to being hurt—well—maybe a bruise or two. What's your name?"

"Lyndon FitzMaurice, from Lancashire. I've just arrived— that is—an hour or so ago."

"And I'm Raymond Betteridge of Betteridge and Henson, stockbrokers."

"I'm glad to know you, sir."

"In the circumstances, I'm even more glad to make your acquaintance. Come, we can't stand here in this downpour. My house is just round the corner."

Lyndon had never been inside such a dwelling before. It seemed to him like a palace with its mahogany furniture, thick carpet and silken drapes at the windows.

Servants ushered him upstairs to a comfortable bedroom, filling a basin with water and laying soft towels and scented soap beside it. They found him clothes to wear, borrowed from one of the younger footmen, and then he was escorted down again to join Betteridge in the dining-room.

Betteridge watched FitzMaurice with interest. Apart from his bravery, the young man was extremely comely and well-spoken. His manners were good and he didn't gobble his food, although it was obvious that he was hungry.

It seemed that he might have come of a good family, yet he had travelled alone from the North. It was a bit of a mystery and Betteridge was intrigued. He asked a few questions but the answers were a trifle evasive. He didn't take umbrage at that; it was a wise man who held his tongue until he knew who his friends were.

"What do you intend to do in London?" Raymond offered wine, which was once more politely refused. Abstinence in a man of tender years was another good sign and he felt himself warming even more to his guest. "Have you made up your mind?"

"I'm going to make money."

The response was bald, uttered in a way which was quite different from FitzMaurice's previous tone. There was cold, implacable resolution there and at first Betteridge was slightly amused.

"I see."

Lyndon met his host's eyes and Raymond stopped smiling.

"When I have enough, I shall go home and right a great wrong done to me."

"How much money will you need?" Raymond knew better now than to chaff the boy. "Will a few hundred pounds do it?"

"No, sir, I'm going to make thousands."

"How? Money doesn't grow on trees."

"I shall make it as you make yours; on the Stock Exchange."

"Do you know anything about about the Exchange?"

"No, but I can learn. I've had a good education. As soon as I've acquired enough capital I'll begin to lend it, at interest."

"Damn it, Fitzmaurice, I believe you will." Betteridge gave a laugh. "Where are you staying?"

"I haven't found anywhere yet."

"If it's not an impertinence, have you any money at

present?"

"Two guineas and a few pence."

"That won't last you for long."

"It won't have to. I shall find work at once."

Raymond leaned back in his chair, his eyes half-closed. He doubted very much whether, at FitzMaurice's age, he would have had the self-confidence to set out from Lancashire to London, with a pittance in his pocket, nowhere to lay his head, and no job in prospect. His respect for Lyndon rose again as wheels began to turn in his head.

"I'll help you," he said finally. "I owe you a favour and I like your spirit. You can stay here tonight, for I wouldn't turn a dog out in this. Tomorrow I'll get you some respectable lodgings and you can start working for me. Normally, the wage wouldn't be much as you've no experience. However, seeing I might be dead but for you, I think I can offer better terms."

He named a figure and a light flickered behind Lyndon's eyes. It had worked out better than even he had dared to hope. Although he firmly believed that he had been meant to go along the street where Betteridge lay helpless, he couldn't deny that the reward was generous.

He was wearing dry clothes, had enjoyed an excellent meal, there was a bed for him to lie in, and he had secured a post in the establishment of a stockbroker. It was as if he himself had designed the plan, leaving destiny to carry it out for him.

"I'm very grateful, sir. I shall do everything I can to ensure that you don't regret your offer."

"It'll take time, but I'll teach you what you need to know."

"And I shall listen to every word you say and act on your advice. I don't intend to be an old man when I return home."

Again Betteridge heard the steel beneath the words and pursed his lips.

"Can you tell me what wrong was done to you?"

Lyndon raised his head and Raymond was shaken by what he saw.

"No, I'm afraid I can't. It's too personal and I don't suppose you'd believe me."

"I think perhaps I would, but I won't press you. One day, when we know each other better, maybe you'll feel able to confide in me."

Lyndon merely nodded. He didn't intend to offend his benefactor by another blunt rebuff. Betteridge had to be nursed and cosseted until all his knowledge and expertise had been wrung from him. He had said he wasn't married, so there was no wife or children to clutter up the situation. He, Lyndon, would become the son Raymond had never had.

In time, he would shew a hint of affection; a few signs of how much admiration he had for his master. He would need to earn more than Betteridge was offering at present, but that wouldn't be too difficult to achieve either. And, if that still proved insufficient there were always other means of obtaining money, but not so clumsily as the two thieves he had driven off.

Although he was bone-tired, Lyndon lay awake for a long time, revelling in the comfort of a feather-bed and blankets made of pure wool. He had no God to whom he could offer thanks, so he addressed his praise to himself.

A good start, he said silently into the darkness. Old Grant put your foot on the first rung of the ladder. Now Betteridge has given you a lift up to the second one. That's about as much help as anyone can expect, Lyndon FitzMaurice. From now on, the rest is up to you.

Sapphire didn't know whether it was her talk with Ashton, or the gift of paper from Mrs Sheldon, which made her decide to tell her father the truth.

Petronella had been encouraging, but Ashton's reaction had surprised her. She wasn't sure which of them was right, but her father would tell her. Besides, she couldn't go on deceiving him any longer.

Decimus listened in silence as she made her confession, rather pale and near to tears when she had finished.

"I didn't mean to disobey you. I knew that if I asked for your permission you wouldn't be able to give it because of the archdeacon. Are you very angry with me?"

Grant stretched out a hand and laid it on Sapphire's head, his own eyes moist. He still thought of her as a child, yet she had had the will and compassion to risk censure to help the small unfortunates who had once come simply for bread and jam. It was her mother all over again.

"No, my dear, I'm not angry," he said gently. "I'm proud of you and what you've done."

"But I was wicked not to tell you."

"I know why you didn't. Still, it would be as well to remember that teaching children to read and write isn't enough. You have to explain right and wrong as well."

"As you did to Donald Grey?"

"No, as I failed to do. Don't follow my bad example. Use your own methods, but make sure they comprehend the Will of God."

Sapphire held her breath.

"Does that mean I may go on as before?"

"It seems a pity to waste Mrs Sheldon's paper, doesn't it?"

"But what will the archdeacon say to you if he finds out?"

"He probably won't; he likes to sleep after luncheon on Sundays, so I'm told. But, if he does, I shall remind him that Our Saviour said: 'Feed my sheep', and He wasn't talking simply of bread and jam."

"Oh, papa, thank you!"

"It is I who should thank you. We learn something new each day, and today I've seen more clearly than ever before that just speaking of how one should do the Lord's work isn't enough. One has to act, as you have done."

Sapphire was silent for a while and Decimus could see that something else was troubling her.

"Another confession?"

She smiled at him, just as Megan did, and his heart was full. He could never understand why so many blessings had been heaped upon him.

"No, I was just wondering, in spite of you letting me continue, whether there was any truth in what Ashton and the archdeacon said. Maybe writing and arithmetic lessons will

61

make some restless and, if that is so, they won't be able to do anything about it. I will have half-opened a door and then slammed it in their faces."

"I don't think so. If I did, I would stop you. When God gave us the ability to learn, he didn't intend our knowledge to be kept locked up inside ourselves. I know most of the children will find scant use for writing, or reading come to that. However, if only one or two out of a hundred benefit from it, then it is worth every moment you spend with them."

"I'm so glad. I needed that reassurance. I shall tell Ashton how wrong he was when I see him again."

"That might not be tactful. I should let the matter drop if I were you. He's quite the stylish gentleman these days, or so I understand."

Decimus caught a glint of something in Sapphire's eyes and saw a slight flush on her cheeks. At first he was alarmed, fearing for her. Then he chided himself for his folly. She was far too young to regard the viscount as anything other than an old playmate. Her blush had been because she thought she had been reprimanded.

As usual, he told Megan all about his day when they retired for the night.

"Did you know what Sapphire was doing?" he asked, watching his wife brushing her satiny hair with long, sweeping strokes.

"Now, there's a thing to ask, and me so busy with my sewing."

He laughed, lying back against the pillows, waiting for her to go to him.

"All right, you've answered me, you minx."

"Haven't called me that for years, have you?" She rose from the dressing-table and got into bed beside him. "Well, *cariad*, minx or not, do you still love me?"

Their eyes met in perfect understanding as she moved into his arms.

"Oh yes, dearest," he said softly. "I love you more than life itself. I really am a very lucky man indeed, aren't I?"

The next morning Sapphire made her way to Hatley Mine, determined to see for herself the conditions which existed in it.

She had been visiting one of her father's bedridden parishioners when she met a tearful Essie Gosling. As she expressed surprise that Essie wasn't at work, the latter had sobbed out the tale of Amy Whalley's death which had taken place not an hour before. Amy had been one of Sapphire's pupils, too, and Essie's description of the frail body, crushed as two of the pit props gave way, had filled her with sorrow and anger.

She left Essie to limp back to the village to tell Amy's widowed mother of the tragedy, having first established where she could find clothes to wear which wouldn't attract attention and thus stop her descent into the mine.

Essie hadn't wanted to tell her where to look, for she was afraid for the Vicar's daughter, but Sapphire had been adamant. In the end, Essie had admitted that there was a hut at the pit mouth where women working on the pit-bank sometimes took shelter in bad weather. Sapphire had learned with disgust that both sexes used the hovel at the same time to change their clothing, but there was no time then for moral squeamishness. If she were fortunate there might be something suitable which she could borrow.

In the event, all that Sapphire could find was a pair of torn trousers and a ragged chemise. They were damp and filthy, but she didn't hesitate as she removed her dress and petticoat, pulling off her stockings and polished boots lest the latter gave her away.

The worker at the top of the pit-shaft barely glanced at her, ordering her to get on the bar attached to the rope. She had expected to go alone, but she found a boy climbing down to join her as they sank crosslapped into the depths of the mine.

She heard the man above cry out a warning that she and her unexpected escort were on their way, a voice from below answering like an echo.

The first thing which struck Sapphire like a blow in the face was the total darkness. Only a single candle held by the boy lit their way as they reached the bottom and were helped from the rope by an overseer.

The second jolt was the silence. The boy and his superior had vanished and Sapphire was alone in a place where it seemed no other human being existed. She began to grope her way along a passage, crouching to avoid the roof, one hand on the wall to guide herself forward. The tunnel appeared to go on forever, but after a moment or two she heard the sound of a door banging and after that some kind of explosion a long way off.

It proved that others were about and her heart began to slow to a normal pace. At the end of the passage she had her first piece of luck. She saw a flicker of a candle and called out to whoever was holding it. She wasn't sure whether she would be heard, or heeded, but then the light drew closer and she took a deep breath as she saw the ghostly face above it.

"Mary! Oh, thank goodness! I thought I was utterly lost and would never find my way out of here."

Mary Formby, a regular attendant at Sunday School, looked at her blankly.

"Miss—Miss Sapphire?"

"Yes, yes, Mary, it's me. Where is everybody?"

"What 'ee doin' 'ere, Miss?"

"Never mind." Sapphire was impatient. "I heard about Amy and I wanted to find out how she met her death. What's that?"

There was a dull, trundling noise which soon faded away into the distance and Mary wiped her nose with the back of her hand.

"It be a corve on way to shaft bottom."

"Shew me where you're working and the others, too."

" 'Ee won't like it."

"I don't suppose I will, but I'm coming with you just the same."

If Sapphire had been alarmed by the dark and quietness, the sight of the women and children in Mary's section of the mine left her dumbfounded.

Females, some young some old, were pulling large baskets up sloping paths, bent almost double because of the low height of the ceiling above them.

"Mary! Those—those women are bare to the waist."

"Aye, nobbut a few wear anythin' a' top of 'em. Too 'ot, you see."

"But it's grossly indecent."

Mary shrugged.

"Men at t'coal face be stark nekkid."

"How awful! But the women don't go near them, do they?"

" 'Course they do. 'Ow else would 'em pick up coal? 'Ere, coom this way."

Round the corner the situation was worse. Boys and nubile females mingled together as they strove to shift the heavy corves. They were sweating and, as Mary put it, chunnering under their breath at their unhappy lot.

"Why have the women got chains between their legs?"

Mary looked at Sapphire pityingly.

" 'Cos they're drawers, o' course. See, them's got a belt round t'waist with chain passin' through legs and fastened to basket. Couldn't move load no other way, could 'em?"

As they got nearer, Sapphire could hear the foul language and coarse jokes being bandied about. Along one adit a man and a girl could be seen struggling in mutual hunger, oblivious to the rocky discomfort which was the setting for their love-making.

Further on still, girls were washing themselves, the men at the opening of the short passage shouting encouragment and lewd advice. The young women, far from resenting either the intrusion or the insults, were yelling back, their comments as base and vile as their male companions'.

When Sapphire saw a miner belabouring a child with a length of wood for not moving quickly enough, she started to run towards him, but Mary held her back.

"Don't be a bluddy fool, Miss. That's Jake Farnworth and 'e's a brute. 'E'd set about 'ee as soon as look at 'ee."

"But the boy can't be more than five." Sapphire couldn't

shake herself free from Mary's grip. "He'll be killed."

"Nay, don't fret 'eself. Us down 'ere don't go that simple. All of us gets beaten if we don't keep up. Men lose money if we be dawdlers."

Shocked to the core, Sapphire gave in, allowing herself to be drawn along another black and seemingly endless passage until they reached the bullstake, or shaft bottom, where the full corves were waiting to be raised to the surface.

It was much lighter in that chamber, for everyone had candles. Sapphire could see more of the grimy walls and roof and the white, haggard faces of those who had just arrived with their loads. So obscene was the conversation which assailed Sapphire's ears that she turned away unthinkingly, running along another tunnel to her right.

Mary wasn't following, but at least she had given Sapphire a stub of wax which she had found by one of the trap doors. Cautiously, Sapphire inched her way along, hoping against hope that her light wouldn't go out. She had no idea where she was, for the eerie silence had wrapped itself round her again. She realised then that she must have strayed away from the place where Mary worked, terrified as she heard the wooden props on each side of her creak ominously.

She was almost in tears, ashamed of her weakness and stupidity in embarking on such a mad escapade. Her presence in the mine would do nothing to help those who strained and sweated there. She hadn't even been able to save a child from a savage thrashing. All that she had done was to endanger her own life and for a moment she leaned against the wall and shut her eyes.

She was ankle-deep in water, her clothes sticking to her, her hands and face caked with coal dust. She didn't think she would ever see the sun or her family again and her prayer was probably the most fervent she had ever uttered.

"Forgive my abominable conceit in thinking I could change things when no one else has been able to do so. My pride and arrogance has led me into this trap, but don't let me die here. I beg you to send someone to help me, even though I don't deserve it. And, dear God, please, please let them come soon! I would so like to go home again."

"Ashton, wait. Look at that poor child. She can hardly walk and is so distressed."

The viscount was out riding with his sister. Minty's companion, Lela Thornley, was bringing up the rear on a mare which made her shake. She had never got used to jolting about in a saddle, but it was all part of the job.

Ashton drew rein as Essie limped up to them.

"My dear." Minty's gentle heart was touched by the pathetic thinness of the girl and her misery. "What is it? Are you hurt?"

As Essie told her story, Rayne felt as if he were turning to stone. Sapphire had gone down his father's pit on her own. Although he had never seen it himself, he had heard enough about it to be filled with dread for her.

"Minty, go home at once."

"But Ashton—"

"I'm going to the mine. I must find Sapphire."

"I'll come with you."

"You most certainly will not. See to this child by all means, but then get back to Lindborough Hall. Miss Thornley, I charge you to see that my sister obeys me."

As he raced away, Minty asked Lela very casually if she would be good enough to wipe the tears from Essie's face. It wasn't an unreasonable request, and Miss Thornley was thankful to be on terra firma if only for a minute or two. Besides, there was nothing in her mistress's tone to indicate that she was being tricked.

She gasped in dismay as Minty struck the mare hard on the rump, making it bolt, and then wheeled round in the direction of Hatley.

"I'm sorry, Lela," she called as she galloped off. "I must help—"

The rest of her apology was lost on Lela and Essie, for Arminta was too far away by then for them to hear her. They looked at each other in consternation, not sure what to do.

"Suppose we ought to tell parson," Essie said doubtfully. "He'll want to know about Miss Sapphire."

"Yes, I suppose we should let him know what's happened. Is it a long walk to the Vicarage?"

"Quite a step. I'm slow; perhaps you'd better go ahead."

"I don't like to leave you."

Essie grimaced.

"I'm used to bein' alone, Miss. I'd rather you hurried on, that's if you don't mind. You see, I loves Miss Sapphire and if summat's gone wrong, she'll want 'er ma and pa. Oh, Gawd! 'Ow I wish I'd never told 'er about Amy Whalley."

Ashton lost no time in establishing that Sapphire had actually gone into the mine. The group round the pit-top were aghast when the fashionable young man flung himself off his horse, announced that he was Viscount Rayne, and then began to shout at them.

The man who had been on duty admitted, under pressure, that a girl with an unusually straight carriage and long, dark hair had been winched down some time ago.

Rayne gave the unfortunate worker a tongue-lashing and then demanded to be lowered himself. At first, no one had wanted to take the responsibility of putting the master's heir at risk, but Ashton's threats soon made them change their minds.

If Sapphire had been appalled by what she had seen in Hately Mine, Rayne was no less shaken. He had crawled painstakingly along one passage after another, jumping aside now and then when a corve trundled along.

He saw the women and children at work, hardly able to believe his eyes. They were like none he'd seen before, alien beings who dwelt underground, no better clad than savages.

The children hurt him most and his lips had thinned to a grim line when finally he reached the crossroads of several tracks. The workers were behind him now; he could hear them in the distance. Close by, however, was the sound of dripping water and timbers shivering uneasily. He realised it was useless to stay there and turned back to try another route.

He prayed that Sapphire wasn't lost in the devilish maze, because one could have stayed there for a week without being found. It was as he was struggling back to where the corves were being pulled up the slopes that he saw Minty and for a moment he couldn't move a muscle. She was on her hands and knees, groping her way forward with her candle, her gown torn and already sodden with water.

But what really made his blood run cold was the black dust which veiled her ash-blonde hair and the creamy pallor of her face. It was as if she were blemished by something which he would never be able to wash away. The fear he had always had about her rose to a point which made his head pound. It was like an omen of what was to come, and at that second he wondered if this was how Minty was going to die, he unable to protect her at the last.

"Minty!" He managed to get to her at last, his voice ragged. "In God's Name what are you doing here? I told you to go home."

She smiled at him and some of the tension eased in him. She wasn't in the least afraid, either of the pit or his ire.

"I've come to help you find Sapphire. Surely you didn't think I'd walk away from her, did you?"

"But I'm here and there are plenty of others about."

"I haven't met anyone else yet."

"They're over to the left. We'd better go and ask them if they've seen anything of her." He paused as a thought struck him. "How on earth did you persuade those men to let you down here?"

"I told them you'd ordered me to follow."

"I'll have something to say to you about this if ever we get out of here."

When Rayne got to the place where he had been watching the drawers at work, he tried to shield his sister from the scene.

"Don't look. It will only upset you."

Minty's amusement at his threat had died away as she looked down at Mary and the others.

"I'm not a piece of fragile glass, Ashton, and this is where

69

Father gets part of his money from. I've always wanted to come down here."

"So have I. Now I wish I hadn't, except to find Sapphire, of course."

"You can't shut your eyes to ugly things. They go on existing, even when people like us wear blinkers. Those children are so young. When I was their age I had two nurses, a suite of rooms at the Hall, and more toys than I had time to play with."

"Don't blame Father too much. I expect every coal mine is much like this. He doesn't force people to come and work for him."

"I don't blame him. I am just wondering what he would say if I stripped myself to the waist and started to pull one of those baskets along."

"Don't, Minty!"

"I'm sorry; I didn't mean to vex you. If Sapphire's been this way I'm sure she will have been noticed."

"I hope so. There are so many tunnels and I'm certain most are unsafe. If she—"

"Now it's my turn to say 'don't'. Come, Ashton, perhaps those women can help us."

It took another hour to find Sapphire. The overseer in that section organized a search and when one small trapper remembered seeing a girl he didn't recognise, they knew in which part of the pit to look for her.

"Sapphire!"

Sapphire turned her head, not able to believe her ears. She just stared at Ashton for a moment or two, trembling as he held out his arms to her. Then she stumbled into them with a cry of relief, her cheeks wet with tears.

Minty held her close while Rayne arranged for a guide to take them back to the base of the shaft.

"You both came." Sapphire held Minty's hand tightly in hers. "I can't take it in. It's dangerous and so very awful. You shouldn't be down here."

"Neither should you be." The viscount's fright had turned

70

to wrath now that Sapphire was safe. "What were you thinking about? How could you be so foolhardy?"

"I came to find out why one of my pupils died this morning."

"I know." Minty was soothing. "We met your Essie Gosling and she told us all about it. Ashton, don't berate Sapphire now. She's upset and as cold as ice. Grumble at her later, if you must, but I understand why she had to come."

"I know I was wrong." Sapphire's voice was shaky. "I deserve to be scolded, especially as my stupidity has put you and Ashton at risk. Minty, dear, forgive me."

"Of course I do, and it's not your fault that I followed Ashton. I wanted to come. Oh good, here's the shaft at last. Now we'll soon be in the fresh air again."

By the time the three of them had been hauled up, the earl and a number of his men had arrived. Stonehurst's face was the colour of parchment and he gave a quick exclamation as he ran forward to catch his daughter as she let go of the rope.

"Minty, my darling, are you all right? Rayne, have you taken leave of your senses? How dared you take your sister down there? She could have been killed."

"Father, I won't have you say a word of reproach to Ashton." Minty's small hand stopped the earl's fury in mid-stream. "He ordered me to go home, but I waited until he was gone and then drove Lela's horse away. She'll confirm that I'm to blame."

The earl lifted Minty in his arms. She was as light as a feather and so delicate to look at. Not for the first time he wished he could lock her way in an ivory tower where nothing could ever harm her.

He turned his head to look at Rayne.

"My apologies, Ashton. But why did you go down?"

"To find me, my lord." Sapphire squared up to Stonehurst, making no attempt to avoid the consequences of what she had done. "All of this is my responsibility. The viscount came to help me; so did Minty. I ought not to have tried anything so reckless, but a girl I knew well was killed down there this morning. I was angry and upset because her life had been so short. Those props shouldn't have given way. Someone was

71

careless."

The earl frowned and Sapphire braced herself against an outburst from his lordship, but it didn't come.

Stonehurst put Minty into the carriage and held out his hand to Sapphire.

"No, you're right. It shouldn't have happened. You'd better come back with us and get cleaned up before your mother and father see you. Crawley, go and find Mr Grant and tell him his daughter is safe and that we'll send her home when we've warmed her up and given her some hot food."

The groom touched his cap and rode off, the earl motioning the carriage forward once Sapphire was safely inside it.

Then he looked back at the viscount. His son's face was sooty-black, but Stonehurst could see the effect his experience had had upon him.

"You didn't like what you saw?" he asked finally, knowing Ashton had to get things off his chest. "You think me callous and unfeeling because of what you found down there?"

Rayne shook his head.

"No, I told Minty it wasn't your fault. I said all mines were much the same and that the people chose to work for you of their own free-will."

"I'm obliged." The earl was dry. "But—?"

"It was hell, my lord." Ashton's voice wasn't quite steady. "Have you been underground lately?"

"No, but I don't need to go. I know what it's like. I'm not making excuses, but that's the way the world is."

"Perhaps, but it shouldn't be, should it? Nothing ought to be as ghastly as that. Father, may we leave now? I've had enough of Hatley for one day. For pity's sake let's go home."

FIVE

On her twenty-first birthday Sapphire Grant sat by the window of her bedroom in Salter's Lodge, thinking about the many changes which had taken place in her life during the past three years.

When Mrs Sheldon had died, her nephew lost no time in seeking a buyer for the Lodge. His haste in trying to rid himself of the property coincided with Mr Wilford Broom's first visit to Lancashire. Having inspected his mine, Bluehill, he had gone on to look at Salter's Lodge and made an immediate offer for it.

He moved in straight away, with his housekeeper, servants and his ward, Matthew, aged five. The landed gentry looked down their noses at him, for he was a mere merchant, but their frosty attitude had bothered him not at all.

When he had paid a courtesy visit to the Vicarage, he had been welcomed with kindness and pleasure, a fact which he never forgot. He played chess with Decimus, complimented Megan on her charms with the utmost propriety, and joked with the younger members of the family as he plied them with sweetmeats.

One day when he was taking tea with Grant and his family, the question of a governess's post for Sapphire cropped up. Sapphire had been Broom's favourite from the start. He nurtured no amorous feeling for her, but her beauty and grace were a constant source of delight to him. He admired her cleverness, which she modestly denied, and the efficient way in which she helped her mother about the house won his whole-hearted approval.

On hearing of the Grants' plans for their eldest daughter he had staked his claim at once. Matthew was the son of old friends of his, both killed in an accident, and Wilford had made up his mind that the child should not suffer in any way because of his loss. A good education was essential and, before she knew it, Sapphire had been installed in Salter's Lodge where she had always longed to live.

But there had been sadder changes as well. A year after she had commenced her duties at the Lodge, Decimus caught a cold. He refused to let Megan fuss and not until his fever was very high had he agreed to take to his bed. Two days later he was dead and Megan, pale but composed, was making plans to return to Wales.

Her father had offered her a home with him, the two girls to be trained as governesses or seamstresses, the boys to go into the butcher's shop to learn the trade. Ivor Jones had been somewhat starchy about it all, because he'd never got over the fact that his daughter had thrown herself away on a pauper.

When Megan and Sapphire parted, the latter said softly: "I wish I could make you look as you did before."

Megan had smiled and patted her daughter's cheek.

"You can't, *cariad*; no one can."

"You miss him so, don't you?"

"We were together for a long time."

"And you loved him."

"I still do; just as much. He hasn't gone far away from me, you know. Perhaps one day it'll be the same for you."

Sapphire had coloured slightly.

"Ashton Howard, isn't it?"

"No, of course not. We are simply—old friends."

"Friends don't make you look like that, lovey. How does he feel?"

"He's engaged to Allene Telford. She's living in France for a year or two, but when she comes back they'll get married."

"There's sadness for you. We both grieve, but at least I had

74

my share of happiness."

Sapphire stirred, the pain of thinking about Ashton almost too much to bear. She didn't know when she had first realised she was in love with him. She thought perhaps she had always been a little in love, even when they'd been young. There had been the magical moment when he had touched her cheek. Then he had taken her in his arms in Hatley Mine and she had known for certain that she wanted him. She remembered how silly she had been about his first show of affection, not happy that their relationship was changing. She wished she could re-live that second or two over again; her reaction would be so different now.

She hardly saw him these days. He was a dashing young blade with a house of his own in London, who returned every so often to Lindborough Hall.

Since she had gone to work for Broom, she had purposely avoided Minty. It wasn't that she didn't care for Arminta any more; she was afraid of embarrassing her by making her acknowledge a mere governess as a friend. She had heard that Ashton would be coming home soon. It had made her heart quicken until she realised how foolish she was being. What was the point of tormenting oneself with thoughts of a man who was to be another woman's husband?

She was thankful when she heard the knock on her door, for she had had enough of memories for the time being.

Wilford Broom came in like a breath of fresh air. He was round and jolly, with iron-grey hair, rosy cheeks and very penetrating blue eyes. He had read the sadness in Sapphire for he was a perceptive man. He didn't think it was brought about just by the death of her father or by pining for Megan. Beautiful young women like Sapphire only looked as she did when they were in love. He felt a sadness of his own, for he had a shrewd idea where her fancy lay.

Even if the aristocracy had no time for him, it hadn't taken him long to cull full facts about them. He knew all about Stonehurst and his family, and had been told of the episode in Hatley Mine when Rayne had risked his neck for Sapphire.

Still, the boy was betrothed elsewhere and there was nothing which he, Broom, could do about it.

"It's almost time for your birthday party," he said, putting aside his regrets. "Matthew can hardly contain himself. He's saved his pocket-money for weeks to buy a present for you."

"Oh, he shouldn't have done."

"For heaven's sake, why not? The boy idolizes you and no wonder, seeing what you do for him. I've got a gift for you, too, and I don't expect a scolding because of it."

"You're so kind to me. I don't know what I'd have done— if—if—"

Wilford was a great believer in changing the subject when females looked as if they were about to cry. He had become very deft in the art over the years.

"Ah yes, there was something I meant to tell you earlier only I forgot," he said quickly. "Our new neighbour, Mr Lyndon FitzMaurice, has just put a very neat one over the earl. Not content with Elstone, the pit he's already got, FitzMaurice has outbid Stonehurst and bought Axby, old Thomas Clegg's mine near Burnley. I'm told the earl is apoplectic and I doubt if he'll be sending FitzMaurice any invitations to his balls and soirées."

Sapphire ignored the reference to the earl, glad to turn instead to the handsome and mysterious stranger who had suddenly appeared in their midst some six months before. Hardly anything was known about him except that he was from London, excessively rich, and had bought a house below Deerpark Moor, spending a small fortune on its renovation.

"I wonder why he wants another mine."

"To make more money, I expect."

"But he's wealthy already, so people say."

"He is; I asked a friend of mine in the City about him. His background is very hazy indeed, but there's no question that his coffers are full."

"There are also rumours that he's not very kind. His workers seem to be frightened of him."

"Oh?"

"Yes, Essie Gosling told me. You remember me mentioning her to you?"

"I remember, but I thought she was at Hatley."

"She is, but a friend of hers works for Mr FitzMaurice. It seems he won't do any repairs, although parts of Elstone are unsafe, especially the bit near the old workings. The laundress who comes here says he's a dangerous man, although how she knows that I've no idea. He keeps himself so much to himself."

"Gossip; servants revel in it. Perhaps he'll come out of his shell before long and give a party. If he invites you, you'll be able to make up your own mind about him."

"If he's unkind, I don't think I want to meet him."

"Then you'll be the only woman in Lancashire who doesn't. Young, rich, good-looking, dangerous—he's out of a romantic novel."

Sapphire laughed.

"Yes, I expect you're right; he will be popular."

Then her smile faded as she looked at Wilford with a frown.

"I wonder—"

"What do you wonder?"

"Whether Mr FitzMaurice would like to buy Bluehill. It's the best for miles and miles."

"It is indeed and it's going to stay that way. I don't intend to face my Maker with the lives of mangled human beings on my conscience through lack of care. In any event, whether he wants it or not he's not going to get it. If he tries any tricks with me, Mr Lyndon FitzMaurice is going to discover very quickly that he's not the only dangerous man around here.

"Now, enough of this exciting gentleman, my dear. Let's go down and put young Matthew out of his misery, shall we?"

A month later Sapphire was riding across the fields towards Worthstone Moor.

The horse she rode was black and sleek, with a fine mane and tail and very knowing eyes. What was even more incredible, he belonged to her.

After she had exclaimed over Matthew's gift of a silver

quill-holder, Broom had demanded that she go outside and look for the present he had bought her. Clues abounded and Matthew had accompanied her, chuckling gleefully as she grew warmer.

She hadn't known how to thank Wilford and, seeing the moisture in her eyes, he had retired hastily to his study saying he had letters to write and that the horse's name was Ambrose.

She had learned to ride when she was quite young, but had never been on the back of such a superb creature as this. She leaned over to whisper an endearment in his ear, hardly noticing that someone was approaching her.

When she heard Ashton call her name she straightened in the saddle. Her first instinct was to turn and use Ambrose's swiftness to save herself unnecessary pain. But when the viscount left his own beast and walked over to her, she knew that however much it hurt she had to stay.

Rayne's feelings were very like Sapphire's. He had long ago understood that the strange emotion which he had felt for her when she was fourteen was love. When he had found her in the mine and she had run into his arms, it was merely a confirmation of his desire for her.

Since the incident at Hatley they had gone their separate ways. He had been at Oxford and, later, tasting the pleasures of London society. On the occasions when he returned to Lindborough Hall he hadn't tried to see Sapphire. It seemed the sensible way to deal with things, yet his decision had left a hollow feeling inside him and the vision of her face never left his mind. There had been one or two casual meetings, but always with Minty or others present. Those hadn't counted. The risk lay in being alone with her and his yearning for her became a sickness which he had to conceal.

"It's been a long time. I haven't seen you since your father died."

"No, it's been quite a while."

"Are you well?"

"Yes, thank you, my lord."

That broke the ice and they both started to laugh.

"Get off that horse, you idiotic wench. Whose is it, anyway?"

"Mine. Mr Broom gave him to me for my twenty-first birthday."

"He has excellent taste in horseflesh. I didn't forget the date, but—"

"I know, Ashton. You don't have to explain."

"No, I know I don't. Minty has missed you. She wonders why you don't go to see her any more."

"I'm a governess. If some of her friends called while I was at the Hall it would be so awkward for her."

"What utter rubbish! You ought to know her better than that."

"I do, really. She's the sweetest, kindest girl in the world. That's why I'm so careful."

"I shall tell her what you've said, so don't be surprised if she comes hammering at Broom's door to take you to task for it."

"There is another reason—that is—I—I—"

He looked at the beautiful colour which had flooded her cheeks and thanked God for what he was seeing. She loved him as much as he loved her, and her blush had betrayed her. It wasn't Minty whom Sapphire was avoiding; it was him.

He lifted her down, keeping his hands round her waist as she hung her head.

He said very gently: "I know what's in your heart because it's the same for me. You don't come to the Hall because you're afraid I might be there."

"That's absurd. I—"

"Don't pretend now; it's too important to both of us. I've got to marry Allene but that doesn't stop me wanting you. Oh, my dear, my dear, I love you!"

Sapphire hadn't realised there could be such wonder in a man's kiss or the feel of his arms tight about one. It was like a dream and one from which she never wanted to awaken. When she had set out from The Lodge she hadn't thought for a second that she'd see Ashton, let alone hear him say the words which set her heart alight. When he let her go she said in a small voice: "Do you want to know whether I love you?"

Ashton was equally amazed at the turn of events. He thought his ride would be a lonely one and, even when he saw Sapphire, he hadn't expected to find courage in himself to admit the truth which had gnawed at him for so long. He laughed, brushing a tendril of her hair from her forehead.

"No, my divine blockhead, I already know. And I hope you're not in the habit of giving such passionate kisses to any man who passes you by."

She shared his laughter, still not quite able to believe what was happening.

"I've never kissed any man before, except father and Mr Broom, when he gave me Ambrose."

"I'm told he's quite elderly."

"Yes, he is."

"Then I forgive you."

They remained silent for quite a while, just holding each other. They didn't need words or protestations of undying ardour; they knew exactly what the other was feeling.

"You know that there can be no more than this, sweetheart, don't you?"

The sadness in his voice made Sapphire put on a brave face for him.

"Of course. Even if Allene didn't exist, your father wouldn't allow you to marry me."

"Probably not, but Allene does exist and I've given her my bond."

"Does that mean we shall never see each other again?"

Her eyes beseeched him and he couldn't resist her.

"Not if you've got the stomach for more clandestine encounters like this. Who can blame two riders if their paths cross? Will you hate me for loving you, kissing you, and holding you close, when I can offer you nothing else?"

"No, dearest, I shall treasure the smallest crumb you have to spare."

"God, Sapphire, why does life have to be so damned unfair?"

"I don't know, but it is. Do you know when Allene is coming

back to England?"

"No, but it won't be for a few months yet. We shall have some time together and we must make every second count, for it's all we shall have for the rest of our days."

"We will, and I shall be riding this way again on Friday afternoon."

He picked up the lightness of her reply. Pouring out his passionate desire for her wouldn't help either of them. She was shewing great courage and he could do no less.

"What an odd coincidence. So shall I."

Their eyes met again, saying what their lips couldn't voice.

"I don't think I ought to come to Lindborough Hall, not even to see Minty."

"You're right, of course." He sighed. "What a difference a few minutes can make to a situation. We don't need anyone else in our world. I'll ask Minty to visit you."

"I'd like that. You won't tell her about us, will you?"

"No, but if she were to see us together she'd know at once."

"Then we must make certain she doesn't see us. Ashton."

"Yes?"

"You could give me my birthday present now, that's if you wanted to. It's late, of course, but I don't really mind."

He took her in his arms, marvelling at what her closeness could do to him. He thought of what it would be like to have her naked in bed with him, closing his eyes to blot out what could never be.

"I haven't got a silver pen-knife this time. Would another kiss be a satisfactory substitute?"

"I can't think of any which would be better. It would be the most splendid gift I've ever had. Oh, my darling Ashton, I do love you so very much."

Six months after he had moved to Deerpark Manor, Lyndon FitzMaurice stood by the window of the morning-room making plans.

No one looking at the tall, elegant man would have thought for a second that he had once been a begrimed trapper in

81

Hatley Mine. His double-breasted frock coat had come from the best tailor in London, the pantaloons cut by a master-hand. He wore a frilled shirt beneath his waistcoat, a satin neckcloth tied very precisely by Curle, his valet.

But the most marked change had been brought about by Nature herself. Three years before, Lyndon had been struck down with a fever, lying ill for several days. When he had recovered sufficiently to get out of bed to bathe his hands and face, he couldn't believe what he saw in the mirror. His hair had turned white, and for a second or two he had been too stunned to move.

Then he had taken another look at the curls dampened by sweat and instantly dismissed any idea of a wig or dye. He doubted if anyone near his former home would recognise him anyway, but the bleached locks were as good as a disguise.

Once he was on his feet again, and had visited his barber, the crisp short hair against slightly tanned skin gave him such a distinguished look that many turned to give him a second glance as he passed by.

In London he had achieved everything he had hoped for, and more. His mind had been quick and receptive and he had learnt the business of stock-broking as easily as he had absorbed Decimus's tutoring. He became indispensable to Betteridge, both as an employee and a close friend, his salary rising steadily as Betteridge's affection for him grew deeper and deeper.

Lyndon had soon started to lend money. He had invested the interest in sound shares and by the age of twenty-one had accumulated a tidy sum. Where business was concerned he had never made the mistake of deviating from the straight and narrow path. He had been wise enough to realise that one whiff of sharp practice and he would be finished in the City.

When he decided he needed to acquire more cash, he had taken to gambling. Once again, his native shrewdness had steered him away from the elite clubs where he would have been denied entry. Instead, he had found smaller places in the seamier parts of London. The stakes were almost as high and one's ancestors were of no importance.

Although he was as lucky at cards as he was on the Exchange, Lyndon's rectitude vanished when he sat down at the tables. If he could win honestly, well and good. When it appeared that he might be losing he hadn't cavilled at cheating, doing it so neatly that no one had ever realised what he was up to.

It was at the Pelican Club near Soho that he met Lord Roger Mitforde and had known intuitively that this was the man he had been looking for.

For several nights he had watched Mitforde lose, seeing the sweat on the latter's brow and the slight tremble in his hands. He had always given generous tips to those working in the Club and it hadn't been difficult to get information about Lord Roger.

Once he had discovered that Mitforde was the black sheep of a noble family, and up to his ears in debt, it had simply been a matter of deciding which approach to use. In the end, when Roger had dropped five thousand pounds in one evening, Lyndon abandoned finesse.

"Will you take wine with me, my lord?" he asked as Roger had lurched from the card table. "I am Lyndon FitzMaurice and I have a proposal to put to you."

Mitforde had been about to brush Lyndon aside as an impudent upstart when he noticed the bag of guineas in FitzMaurice's hand. He had sat down abruptly on the nearest chair, sensing a way out of his dire predicament.

"What sort of proposal?" Mitforde hadn't taken his eyes off the money. "Not illegal, is it?"

"No more than cheating at cards or failing to pay one's gambling dues."

"Damned impertinence!"

Lyndon had smiled.

"I saw you; you're an amateur. You should watch me and see how I do it."

Lord Roger had remained very still while the waiter poured the wine and then discreetly withdrew.

"Well?" he asked finally. "What do you want of me?"

"I'm glad you're astute enough to see that I do have a need of your services."

"Naturally I see it. You want to buy me, I presume. For what purpose and what price do you put on my head?"

"You cannot give me blue blood, but you can teach me everything else I need to know to enable me to become a gentleman. Don't worry; I shan't remain in town for much longer. I will cause you no embarrassment by tapping on doors which are locked against me. As to my valuation of you—well—shall we say a down payment of one thousand guineas and a loan of a further four?"

With his unerring instinct for using the right tool at the right time, Lyndon settled down to a new kind of scholarship. Mitforde had not merely been grateful for Lyndon's unstinting generosity; he liked his pupil as well. Furthermore, he had understood at once that Lyndon lived in two separate worlds.

By day FitzMaurice moved in the London money markets. At night he frequented the darker side of Soho. Once told what Lyndon's business was, Roger had never mentioned it again. At the end of two years there was nothing left for FitzMaurice to learn, and Mitforde was solvent for the first time in years.

Lyndon had continued to accrue money, making a quick killing on the market now and then, but never quite achieving the kind of capital he really wanted.

The turning point had come when Betteridge died of a stroke. Lyndon found that his benefactor had left him everything he possessed, including his partnership in the firm. Raymond had been a good deal richer than FitzMaurice had realised, and he could have settled for what he had. But something had driven him on, as if it had to be his own hand and mind which took him to the heights for which he aimed.

He had used half of his assets in one final, and apparently wild, speculation. His peers had shaken their heads, forecasting his ruin. Secretly they had all hoped he would crash, for the very self-assured young man had come too far too quickly for their taste.

The gamble had paid off and Lyndon had laughed quietly to himself as he bought out his partner before returning to Lancashire for a while.

Once he had found Deerpark Manor, Lord Roger had done the rest. Mitforde had known exactly whom to engage to repair and decorate the beautiful seventeenth-century house, and where to acquire the best furniture, carpets, curtains and paintings. It was Roger who had hired the staff and told Lyndon how to handle them, and who purchased the thoroughbreds for the stables. But his most useful effort on FitzMaurice's behalf had been the introduction to the latter of Stanley Curle.

Curle was a good deal more than a valet. His mind was almost as devious as Lyndon's own and scruples were things he didn't recognise. The two men had felt an immediate affinity for each other. Lyndon paid Stanley a ludicrously high wage and in return got total loyalty and devotion.

Curle didn't bat an eyelash when he had been asked to hire men from the Yorkshire pits to cause accidents in the Earl of Stonehurst's mine. He had merely inclined his head, taken the large sum held out to him, and gone off to make the necessary arrangements.

There had been four quite serious incidents since Lyndon had returned and Curle reported rather smugly that his lordship was growing very worried.

When Thomas Clegg decided to sell up, it was Curle who found out what Stonehurst was offering, thus enabling Lyndon to better the price and get Axby.

"His lordship is mightily put out," Stanley had told Lyndon, when all the documents had been signed. "He's been negotiating for some months, I believe."

"Serves him right." FitzMaurice had shrugged. "He should have raised his bid. If you really want something in this world, you have to pay for it. Always remember that."

Curle assured his master that he would, and then went to enquire about the Reverend Decimus Grant and the Grey family, asking no questions nor even shewing a vestige of

85

interest. Men Like Lyndon FitzMaurice didn't like nosey servants.

Lyndon had been relieved to discover that what was left of his adoptive family had moved away, and that Grant was dead. Now there was no one who could pose a threat to him as he began to consider a scheme for the earl's destruction.

He had deliberately kept himself hidden for a while, knowing full well what speculation and intrigue would be aroused by such a ploy. He hadn't expected the aristocracy to call on him, and those of lesser importance on the social scale who ventured to his front door were told very firmly that the master wasn't 'at home'.

He turned from the window as Stanley Curle came padding into the room. He was a small, lithe man who moved with the sinuous grace of a cat. He was fastidious in the matter of dress and as greedy for money as Lyndon had been.

"Yes, what is it?"

"It's your Elstone mine, sir. Joe Bricker, the manager, is here."

There were ugly lines at the corners of FitzMaurice's mouth.

"He has dared to come here—to my home?"

"He's an ignoramus, but seems very anxious about the state of parts of the roof. He says that if something isn't done at once, there could be a collapse. Do you want me to give him the order to proceed?"

"Certainly not." Lyndon was indifferent to the safety of his employees. The Earl of Stonehurst hadn't cared a button for those who toiled at Hatley and it was another lesson which Lyndon had learned well. "I'm not going to waste good money on Elstone; it's almost exhausted. That's why I bought Clegg's colliery and why I want Broom's. If the men don't like the conditions, let them go and work elsewhere."

"Yes, sir. What shall I tell Bricker?"

Stanley wasn't surprised at his master's response. The fact that he served FitzMaurice with unflagging zeal didn't blind him to the kind of man he was dealing with. He passed no

86

judgements. All he was concerned with was the size of his own bank balance.

"Tell him to go to hell and that if he bothers me again with trivialities he'll be out of a job. And, Curle—"

"Sir?"

"I think it's time I came out of my retreat. I suspect I've whetted my neighbours' appetite for a sight of me long enough, don't you agree?"

"Indeed." Curle permitted himself a feline smile. "The ladies will be delighted. From what I hear they're all agog to see you."

"Especially the mothers of plain and unmarried daughters."

"You are something of a temptation to them, if you will forgive me for saying so."

"I expect I am, but I didn't come back to tie the knot with some bucolic female. Nevertheless, we'll have a grand party and satisfy their curiosity. See to everything, will you? Make sure no names are left off the invitation list."

The valet hesitated, not sure how to issue his warning without giving offence.

"Yes, sir, but of course there will be a few who won't accept."

Lyndon's eyes were blank, hiding his thoughts from his servant. In most things he was free with his confidences to Stanley, not bothering about the fact that Jennings, the butler, wasn't allowed to do his job because Curle preferred to deal with callers himself in case he missed something. This time, FitzMaurice wasn't quite ready to say any more and he shrugged.

"The earl and his cronies, you mean? Well, let them stay away. It's all one to me. Plenty of others will come, so your efforts won't be wasted. Don't stint on anything. Get more footmen and maids; spend as much as you like. I shan't count the cost. This is going to be one ball which everybody around here will remember for the rest of their lives.

"Oh yes, m'dear fellow. Now we're really going to make them sit up and take notice."

Ashton and Sapphire met as often as they could. Their favourite spot was Brierly Wood and they were blissfully happy together, coming gloriously alive as they held each other close, their lips touching.

One particular afternoon Sapphire was resting her head against Ashton's shoulder, wishing time could stand still, when he spoke quietly.

"Of course you'll marry eventually, won't you? I can't bear to think of another man possessing you, but that's because I'm selfish. I can't make you my wife and I've no right to stand in your way."

She twisted round to look at him, seeing his despair.

"No, I shan't marry. How could I if the man wasn't you?"

"But you'll be so lonely."

"Better to be lonely than have to live with a man one hates. And I would hate him, you know, because he'd tried to take your place. Don't worry about me. I shall have the memory of our weeks together to comfort me."

"Such a short span to last a lifetime."

"It will be enough, dearest."

"It'll be terrible when we meet, after my wedding, I mean."

"I don't suppose we shall meet."

"Not alone, naturally, but you're Minty's friend. There are bound to be a few occasions when we find ourselves attending some function or other."

"I doubt it; I'm only a governess. I shan't move in your circle any more than I do now."

He didn't seem to hear her, too wrapped up in the bleak future.

"I don't know what I will do. I'll want to take you in my arms and tell you how much I've missed you."

Sapphire grieved for him and for herself, but she tried to be severely practical.

"Then we must avoid such encounters. It would be painful for me, too. I'm not sure that I could stop myself saying how deeply I love you."

Ashton caught hold of her, his grip almost savage.

"Sapphire, I need you so much. I wish Broom would go back to London and take you with him. Then I wouldn't have to live with temptation so close to me. Did you really mean what you said just now? Would you truly forsake companionship, security, and children, for me?"

"I meant it. No other man will ever touch me. I'll be yours alone, wherever we are. I'll close my eyes and remember you just as you are now. No one can take that away from me."

"As the years go by I shall become old and crochety. I expect I'll go bald and get fat into the bargain."

Her eyes filled with tears.

"Perhaps, but I won't be there to see the changes, will I? To me you'll always be young and strong and the most handsome man I've ever known."

They forgot about words, their mouths making anguished pleas which they knew could never be granted.

Lyndon FitzMaurice watched them. He had been walking in the wood when he had caught sight of them. As soon as he had returned, he had made it his business to observe Rayne without the latter seeing him. It hadn't been difficult with Curle's help.

He remembered the girl, too. Once she had come into St Luke's church, calling to her father. He had got up and peered through the slightly open door of the vestry. She hadn't changed all that much. The child's body had matured miraculously into a woman's rich curves, but the long, black hair, dark eyes and radiant complexion were the same.

He had crept forward stealthily when they had started to talk, concealing himself behind thick gnarled trunks. They were too lost in themselves to notice anyone else, and his smile was cold and satisfied.

It had always been his intent to punish Stonehurst's son and daughter as well as the earl himself. Curle had told him that the viscount was engaged to Lord Telford's daughter, now abroad for a while. FitzMaurice had no idea whether Ashton Howard and Sapphire had a sexual relationship, nor did he care. The important thing was the viscount's undoubted passion for the girl in his arms.

The idea flashed into his mind at once. He would take Sapphire Grant by force. He would despoil and degrade her and then throw the sordid facts into Howard's face. Until that moment he hadn't been sure how to injure Ashton. But, as usual, he had been lucky. He now knew his enemy's Achilles' heel; the rest would be easy.

For a brief moment, as he walked silently back to where he had left his horse, he thought of all that Decimus Grant had done for him.

Then he brushed the matter aside. The parson had been weak. If he had been fool enough to waste his time on a common pit-boy, that was his affair.

Yes, indeed, my lord, he said under his breath as he mounted up. First you, then your spoilt sister, and finally Stonehurst. I'll break the lot of you before I'm through. I wonder if our good father will ever tell you why."

SIX

Not long after Essie Gosling had become a drawer she met Tobias Locket.

He was a miner who worked at the coal-face, lying on his side as he hacked away with a sharp pick. When Essie had come to fill her creel, he had given her a friendly grin, stopping his labours long enough to roll the lumps and nuggets into the basket shaped like a cockle-shell, flattened at the neck.

But when he had seen how thin she was, and how she dragged one leg, the smile had died away in mute anger. A strap was placed round the bottom of the basket, then stretched over the bearer's forehead to ensure the load was secure. In order to tighten the arch thus formed, the body had to bend into an almost semi-circular position.

Tobias had felt impotent rage as he saw Essie's furrowed brow and grimed cheeks stained with sweat. He had wanted to help her, but of couse that had been impossible. His place was at the long-wall working; she had to make the lengthy and hazardous journey to the bullstake.

"That be too heavy for you."

Essie tried to look at him, but it was difficult weighed down

91

as she was.

"I can carry it; 'ave to, don't I?"

"Ain't right, though. Not woman's work."

"Most bearers 'ere be women and girls, 'adn't you noticed?"

"Still wrong. Looks like you'll snap in two."

She had managed to laugh.

"I'm stronger 'un I look. I'll manage, allus 'ave, but thanks anyway."

After that, they had a brief chat on each of Essie's trips and at the end of twelve months were much in love. Marriage seemed out of the question. Essie's mother still lay helpless on her mattress and Lucy had developed tuberculosis and couldn't work.

Tobias's plight was almost as bad. Like Essie, he had lost his father and brothers in a pit disaster and was left with a nagging shrew of a mother who took all his wages from him.

In spite of the hopelessness of their respective situations, they still dreamed. They talked as if it was only a matter of time before they became man and wife, even discussing how they would furnish their cottage when they got one. Both knew such fantasies would never materialise, but it helped to get them through the long, hard days.

One morning when Essie arrived at the face, Tobias saw she had been crying. Full of concern he twisted round and knelt beside her.

"What's up, luv?"

"Nothin'."

"People don't cry for nothin', 'specially you. Come on, out wi' it."

Essie still hesitated, not wanting to burden him with any more troubles. In the end she gave way, for she could see he wouldn't give up until she'd spoken.

"Our Lucy's worse. Coughed all night and brought up blood."

"Poor little beggar. Can't no one 'elp 'er."

"Don't think so, not now. It's too late. We've never 'ad the money for medicines and such like."

"She got enough to eat?"

Essie didn't look at him.

"Reckon so."

"Tell us truth, lass."

"Well, I bought 'er a blanket last week 'cos she were shiverin' so. Didn't leave much over. I gave 'er my share and she ain't that 'ungry."

Tobias ground his teeth, hating the earl who probably threw away more food in a day than Essie and her family saw in a month. He fished in the pocket of the jacket he had discarded and brought out a few coppers.

" 'Ere, take this. Get Lucy some milk or summat."

"Can't take it off you, Toby. What 'ud your ma say?"

Essie knew all about Mrs Locket and her sharp tongue although she'd never met her. She and Tobias had no secrets from each other and from time to time he was glad to let off steam about his rapacious mother.

"She won't know."

" 'Course she will. Money'll be short."

"I'll tell 'er I dropped it."

"She'll be that cross. You'll be fratchin' all evenin'."

"I'll go out; let 'er talk to t'walls for a change."

Essie took the offering, tucking it into her belt.

"It's that good of you, Toby."

"Don't be daft. I loves you."

"I loves you, too."

" 'Ow about a quick kiss then afore I lift this bluddy basket on thee back?"

"Someone might see us."

"Don't care if they does. What's one kiss against what most of t'men and their doxies get up to down 'ere?"

Their lips touched and Essie sniffed, trying not to weep again.

"Come Sunday, what about you and me walkin' out for a while?"

Her heart leaped in joyous anticipation.

"Could we?"

"Why not? Yer ma 'ud let you go, wouldn't she?"

"Aye, but what about yours?"

"I shan't mention that either. Let 'er guess where I am. Essie, meet me by the edge of Throcketts Wood at two, eh?"

She nodded, not caring any more about the tears which rolled down her cheeks.

"Yes, Toby; oh, yes! Two o'clock by t'old beech tree. Wish it were Sunday tomorrow. It's goin' to be the 'appiest day of me life."

Wilford Broom had been away when Lyndon FitzMaurice's ball took place, and Sapphire was confined to bed with a heavy cold. Upon his return, Wilford decided to throw his own party. In spite of what she had said, he knew that Sapphire wanted a glimpse of the new master of Deerpark Manor, but not nearly as much as he did.

FitzMaurice had got hold of Axby by a ruse. Broom always liked to size up his adveraries in advance, and he had had no illusions about his neighbour. One day, FitzMaurice was undoubtedly going to be an opponent.

The invitation to the Howards was addressed to Minty, a note from Sapphire tucked inside saying she would understand if Minty couldn't come. When Minty received it she hid it, saying nothing to the earl who was about to go to London, or to her brother, just setting off for Somerset. The family had an estate there and, reluctant as the viscount was to leave Lancashire, he had had to agree to his father's request that he should attend to a problem which had arisen over certain rights of way. To refuse would have aroused suspicion and might have led to an end of his meetings with Sapphire.

After Stonehurst and Ashton had gone, Minty approached her aunt, Lady Dorothea Henderson. Lady Dorothea had arrived to look after Arminta in the earl's absence. She was elderly, short-sighted, and getting deafer by the day. However, she was of very exalted lineage and her name was more than sufficient to protect Minty's reputation. The small army of servants could do the rest.

When her niece had explained about the party to be given by Wilford Broom, Lady Dorothea was receptive.

"Broom—Broom? Ah, yes; one of the Devonshire Brooms, of course?"

Minty's reply had been mumbled and her aunt took it to be one of confirmation. Arminta didn't like deluding her august relative, but Ashton had told her why Sapphire had been keeping away from the Hall. That, together with the note from her friend, made it important for Minty to attend the party, just to shew Sapphire that she still loved her.

Lyndon's prediction had been right. His ball had made people sit up and take notice, and it was still talked about whenever a few women got together for a gossip. They exclaimed over the magnificence of the Manor, the excellence of the wine and food, the skill of the musicians who played for the dancers, and, most of all, about Lyndon himself. He had set many a mother praying, and every girl over sixteen had fallen in love with him on the spot.

He had been a perfect host, but just remote enough to cause more flutterings in the female bosom. His lips smiled but his eyes did not, and over the tea-cups it was agreed readily that Mr FitzMaurice could indeed be regarded as dangerous. It was a delicious topic and speculation grew hotter and hotter, everyone wanting to be invited to Broom's soirée when word got about that Lyndon would be there.

Broom hadn't stinted either, but he made no attempt to emulate the lavishness of FitzMaurice's ball. It wasn't his way and, if he had to get the better of the newcomer, it would be in business not over a social gathering.

Lyndon accepted the invitation, partly to see what sort of opposition Broom would present, and partly to get to know Sapphire. In order to get near enough to rape her, he had first to become acquainted with her. He met Broom's straight, shrewd eyes, making a mental note not to underestimate him, and then turned to study Sapphire.

Beautiful though she was in her white gown, she left him totally unmoved. He thought perhaps that was just as well in

95

the circumstances. Even the mildest emotion would get in the way of what he was going to do. He put himself out to be particularly charming to her, claiming three dances and drawing envious glances down on Sapphire by his attentiveness.

He was about to make his adieux, having broken the ice with his prey, when Broom approached him again accompanied by a girl in yellow silk.

As soon as Lyndon looked at Arminta's face he knew something tumultous had befallen him. He stared at her ethereal loveliness, feeling his heart hammering with such force that it seemed it might stop beating at any moment.

Lord Roger hadn't neglected the normal appetites of his apprentice. Lyndon had met many glamorous women, some of high birth, others of the *demi-monde*. He had slept with them and left them in the morning without a single regret.

When Broom announced his companion as the earl's daugther, FitzMaurice turned cold. He had already made up his mind what he was going to do with her. His intent towards Arminta Howard was the same as that in store for Sapphire Grant, but with one important difference. Arminta was his half-sister and Stonehurst would be faced not only with a ruined daughter, but a small matter of incest into the bargain.

Not for a second had he expected anything to crop up to alter his plans. He hadn't seen Arminta before, nor had he really given her much thought. Now she was there, a few feet away from him, smiling in a way which made him light-headed.

Minty had heard all the rumours and tales of FitzMaurice, but hadn't paid much attention to them. In her sheltered world only a few, very carefully chosen young men were allowed to enter. She hadn't realised that the man everyone was talking about was to be at Broom's that evening. Even if she had done so, it wouldn't have meant a great deal to her. She had only come for Sapphire's sake.

Now, as she looked at him, she felt a curious sense of contentment. She hadn't been aware of anything lacking in her life until that moment. Then, when FitzMaurice had got his breath back and asked her to dance with him, she realised how empty her days and nights had been.

She slipped her hand into his, and both knew at once that it belonged there. Their eyes remained locked as smoothly they moved on to the floor to take part in the quadrille.

After a while he asked a question. He already knew the answer to it but he wanted to hear her voice again. It was like soft, seductive music and he knew he would never be able to hear enough of it.

"Are the earl and viscount with you?"

"No, they're away."

"Surely you didn't come on your own?"

Her gentle laugh was even more bemusing and he was hurting inside as he had never done before.

"No, of course not. My aunt, Lady Dorothea Henderson, is accompanying me. She should have been introduced when I was, but she stopped to talk to one of the footmen under the impression that he was Lord Conran. She's a dear, but rather woolly these days."

"I'm glad. If she wasn't, I might find myself dancing with her instead of with you."

He hadn't meant to say that, for the girl who had cast an instant spell over him was a stumbling block in the path of revenge. He was about to mouth some more conventional observation about the party when Minty spoke quietly.

"You don't have to make any more small-talk. We both know what's happened."

He felt his mouth dry as he looked down at her.

"Do we?"

"Of course. You can pretend otherwise for a while longer, if you want to; I don't mind. Lela, my companion, has a very weak will and is remarkably accommodating. My favourite ride is out to Hambledon Hill. I go there every morning."

The fear in him was growing and he tried to fight it by keeping silent. When the music stopped, Minty curtsied in response to his bow.

"We mustn't dance together again. People will notice us.

97

You won't forget, Lyndon, will you? When you're ready—Hambledon Hill."

As she floated away, light as thistledown, Lyndon helped himself to a drink and went out on to the terrace. He had to be alone for a few minutes to gather his scattered thoughts together and recover from the fatal blow he had received.

He looked at the night sky and told himself that he had imagined the violent turbulence which had struck like a thunderbolt. He wasn't in love with the earl's daughter, and there was nothing to stop him pursuing his plan. He repeated the comforting reassurance over and over again, but they were just so many empty words churning about in his head. All that was real to him was the sound of his name on Arminta Howard's lips.

In the end he had to go inside again. Every move he made was being noted by the matrons who were trying to catch his eye. Nothing must appear unusual. He had to be as cool and detached as ever, or he might give himself away.

He swore to himself for thinking along those lines. There was nothing to give away. He had merely taken a turn round the floor with a young woman whose life he was about to wreck. But even before the profanity was finished, he knew one thing for certain. The fragile creature, with intoxicating beauty of face and form, had just turned his whole existence upside down. However many times he denied it, sooner or later he would have to admit the truth.

He had met Arminta Howard and touched her hand, and he would never be the same man again.

Lyndon had never intended to fake love or courtship with Sapphire Grant. He had heard enough about her to realise that she was too sensible to be taken in that way. Curle had discovered that she was something of a scholar and still taught in Sunday School, wrestling with simpletons who had no capacity for learning.

As he was musing on the best way to gain her full attention and trust, Curle had remarked off-handedly that the room she used for her classes had a leaky roof and broken windows. Lyndon had smiled, for it was the perfect answer. Sapphire would be full of praise if he bought a place to be set aside for the education of the young. She would be eager to see it and wouldn't see the trap until it had closed on her.

After his meeting with Arminta he couldn't have managed anything like a real friendship with another woman. Although he still hadn't ridden out to Hambledon Hill, or accepted what his half-sister had said, no whisper of a liaison, however innocent, must reach Arminta's ears.

Stanley acquired an old house about a mile or so away from Salter's Lodge. Once it was his property, Lyndon began to watch Sapphire's movements, calculating the most propitious time and place to approach her.

He decided that after her Sunday class would be the best opportunity. She walked from St Luke's to the Lodge on her own, having said goodbye to the grubby children who clustered round her.

When Sapphire saw Lyndon coming towards her she felt no alarm. As she had told Wilford after the soirée, she hadn't taken to FitzMaurice, yet she could see no harm in him. When he raised his hat she returned his greeting, trying to guess what he wanted of her.

"A new school!" She forgot all about her doubts as her eyes shone with delight at his announcement. "You have actually bought a house for me to use?"

"Yes, for you and for the sons and daughters of the poor. They need our help."

In her excitement she missed the irony in FitzMaurice's voice and when he suggested they should go and look at the house, she agreed at once. She wasn't like Minty, having to be guarded against any breath of scandal. She was a working girl and it would have been churlish to refuse to go with FitzMaurice after his generosity.

It did occur to her that it was rather hidden and isolated, but she pushed the criticism away. It didn't really matter where the house was as long as she could fill it with children.

99

It was very cold inside, as if it had been locked up for a long time. It was dirty, too, but again Sapphire scolded herself. Mr FitzMaurice had been good enough to purchase it; one couldn't expect him to get down on his knees and scrub the floors as well.

It wasn't until they mounted the stairs and entered a room which still had blinds at the windows that Sapphire felt her first real twinge of fear.

The window covering was torn and enough light came through to shew that there was a bed in one corner, apparently the only piece of furniture in the place. It didn't look at all old, or grubby either. She turned quickly and the colour drained from her face as she saw Lyndon's expression.

"Yes, you're quite right, Miss Grant. I'm not interested in the vermin from the mine. They can stay ignorant for the rest of their lives as far as I'm concerned. It's you I want."

"I—I don't understand."

Sapphire wasn't a weakling, but she knew at once that there was no chance of getting away from FitzMaurice.

"Don't you?" Lyndon was trying not to think about Arminta. "It's really quite simple. I need a woman."

"You're—you're mad! Why do you want me? There are many who would be only too glad to become your mistress."

"Ah, but I don't want them."

"Nor do I want you. Mr FitzMaurice, let me pass. You're being quite ridiculous and I won't—"

When he pulled the hat from her head and the shawl from about her shoulders, Sapphire began to fight. She clawed at him, kicked him, bit his hand, and tried to thrust him away with her knee. It was quite useless and as he tore the front of her dress open she knew she was beaten.

He threw her down on the bed and laughed at her, calling her a gullible fool. Where her face should be, he could see Arminta's, and amusement gave way to insensate rage. It should have been Arminta there in his arms. It ought to have been her flesh he was stroking, her ear into which he whispered things about passion.

100

He had no compunction in taking Sapphire Grant when he was ready; his only misgiving was because he was soiling his hands on another woman. After meeting Arminta, he should never have done that, but the plan had been made a long time ago. It was the first blow against the Howards, and the viscount would be livid when he heard about Sapphire's romp.

Rayne would never believe that she had gone into an empty house with a man she had only met once, unless it was for immoral purposes. He would deny ownership of the property, for Curle already had his instructions to sell it. He would also deny his promise to provide a new school, leaving Sapphire a liar and a trollop.

Sapphire hit out at her attacker for as long as she could, exhausted as finally FitzMaurice lost patience and penetrated her with callous brutality.

When Lyndon rolled off the bed and stood up, Sapphire made for the door, trying to pull the edges of her torn dress together. She knew he was following her; she could hear his footsteps on the stairs as she ran outside screaming.

Then she was conscious of two dreadful things happening at the same time. FitzMaurice had caught up with her, stripping the gown down to her waist. At precisely the same moment she looked up and saw Ashton.

She hadn't realised that he had returned from Somerset, but there he was, riding a chestnut horse. Her mouth was opening to beg him for help when she saw the look in his eyes.

His gaze wandered over her from top to toe, distain straigtening the line of his lips. She tried to call out to him and tell him that he was wholly wrong in what he was thinking, but the words wouldn't come. The saliva had dried in her mouth, and she began to see herself as Ashton was seeing her.

Her hair had fallen loose from its pins, her cheeks were flushed, and she was half-naked. She knew that FitzMaurice had let go of her, but it was too late. The harm was done and the viscount gave her one last contemptuous stare as he turned his horse's head and rode off like the wind.

"You devil! You heartless, wicked devil!"

She turned to rend FitzMaurice tooth and nail, but he had gone as quickly as Ashton. She didn't go back to collect her hat and shawl. She never wanted to see the house again and she raced back to Salter's Lodge as fast as she could, praying she wouldn't meet anyone on her way.

In that she was fortunate and she fell on her bed, racked with sobs which shook her whole body.

Broom heard her and hurried in. He saw the state she was in and knew at once what had happened. It only remained for Sapphire to tell him who was responsible. Wilford held her in his arms until she was quieter, then he brushed the damp hair from her face and said gently:

"You're safe now, my dear, quite safe. Who did this to you?"

"I can't—I can't—"

Wilford was very firm.

"You must. I want his name."

"It was—no—I can't—"

"Do you want me to assume it was Rayne? I know he's back."

He saw the agony in her at the mention of the viscount and then she submitted, the stuffing knocked out of her.

"I'll kill him." Broom whispered the words, but they were no less deadly for all that. "I'll kill the bastard."

"No, no, you mustn't!" Sapphire clutched at Wilford's hand, her fears renewed. "No one must know about this, don't you see? The only person who saw me was the viscount and he won't say anything. I ought to tell you about Ashton, too, I suppose."

When she had got to the end of her story, Broom held her against him once more.

"My poor child, my poor child. Rayne should be told the truth."

"He wouldn't believe it," she replied drearily. "He saw me as I am now, with FitzMaurice's hands on me. Nothing would ever convince him that I was innocent. FitzMaurice said I was gullible, and he was right. How stupid I was to imagine for a moment that he had bought a school to help the miners'

102

children. He isn't that sort of man, is he?"

"I'm not sure just what sort of animal he really is, but not a philanthropist, I agree. I want him, Sapphire, and I'm going to get him."

"No, no, please, please don't! If you approach him, he would deny it, or say that I was willing. Then Matthew and everyone else would find out. For my sake, please let it be. I understand your anger, and I'm grateful for it, but the only way you can help me is to keep my secret."

After a moment or two Broom nodded. He saw the sense of what Sapphire was saying and he didn't want her hurt any more. Rayne's scorn must have been worse than the rape, for Wilford had seen the look in Sapphire's eyes when his name was spoken. He, Broom, couldn't add to her torment just because he had never been so angry in all his life.

"All right," he said at last. "I won't do anything, at least not for a while. However, there is another way in which I can help you."

Sapphire shook her head.

"I don't really think there is."

"Will you always love Ashton Howard?"

"With all my heart, but I can never have him. Even before this happened he was beyond my reach. He's going to marry Allene Telford."

"Then you have nothing to lose by marrying, too."

"Marrying?" She stared at Wilford blankly. "Who would want me as a wife after what took place today?"

"I do."

He saw her reaction and patted her cheek.

"Don't worry, it's only my name and protection that I'm offering you. I'm far too old and lazy to play the husband, and I don't want a woman's perfume and powder cluttering up my bachelor's bedroom."

Sapphire was still numb. The terror of that afternoon was still as vivid as ever. Now Wilford had stunned her yet again.

"But that would just be pity."

"Nonsense; it would be nothing of the sort. You must know

103

how very fond I am of you."

"But fondness isn't love."

"No, it's a poor substitute, I agree, but it makes no demands. I'll give you comfort and security for the rest of your days. You will never have to be concerned about money, or a roof over your head, and you'll lighten the last few years of my life as no one else in the world could do."

"You are so very kind and I love you as well. Not as I—"

"No, of course not. I know where your heart lies. Well, what do you say?"

She was still doubtful.

"What if—that is—suppose I were to have a baby?"

Broom gave a laugh.

"That would give my friends something to think about, wouldn't it? If there should be a child, I will acknowledge it as mine. Don't upset yourself too much about that; it may not happen. Marry me, Sapphire. Let me look after you, as your father would have wanted me to."

Sapphire thought about it a minute or two longer, then she nodded. Her father was dead, her mother a long way away, and she herself was out of Ashton's life for good.

That night as she lay in bed, still bruised and battered by her experience, she wondered what Megan would have said. Her mother had written many letters. At first they were quite sad, and it was clear that Grandfather Jones's charity was somewhat chilly. Then, gradually, his thawing came through in the lines her mother wrote. There was no longer any talk of the girls being trained to be governesses. They were to go to Europe with Ephraim and Shem, now considered too good to be in the butchering business.

Only a week ago another letter had come. Grandfather had taken a villa in Rome for a year.

"*Imagine it,*" Megan had written in her untidy scrawl.

> "*Almost next door to the Pope and me brought up strict Chapel. Your grandpa wanted to send word to you to join us, but I put him off. Thought Ashton Howard might have the sense to change his*

mind. If you want to come, cariad, *just say so; we'd love to see you, you know that.*

"*How I wish my dear Dessy could see me in my new gowns and gew-gaws. Still, perhaps he'd think me flighty and drag me off to a museum to improve my mind.*

"*Always knew my father had a penny or two tucked away; never dreamed anyone could make so much out of cutting up pieces of meat.*"

Sapphire had smiled when she had received the missive; she wasn't smiling any more. She would have to write and explain to her mother that she was going to marry Wilford Broom and hope against hope that Megan wouldn't ask why.

The world was a cold, hard place. She had realised that when she had seen Hatley Mine. She closed her eyes, trying to forget that occasion for it was then that Ashton had taken her in his arms for the first time.

Doing good to others didn't bring its own reward, as her father had always said it would. Because she had wanted something better for the children she had gone with FitzMaurice to that dark house. She had lost her virginity and she would never be whole again.

She made up her mind that in future she would hit out first, before others could strike a blow at her. She would become steely and uncaring as the man who had stolen what should by rights have been Ashton's.

She heard the tap on the door and bade the knocker enter. It was Wilford, and she recalled that once before he had come to her room and driven away unhappy memories. He was doing it again now, with a cup of hot chocolate and a compassionate smile.

"I saw your light and guessed you wouldn't find it easy to sleep. Drink this, and then try to get some rest. It's been a harrowing ordeal for you, but you've got to put it behind you if you can. God, I wish I could get my hands on—"

"You promised you wouldn't." Hastily, Sapphire sat up, her hand reaching for Broom's. "You said—"

"I know what I said. Don't fret; I'm not going after him with a gun, giving the game away, but you may be sure of this. One of these days, Lyndon FitzMaurice is going to rue what he did to you. He read me wrongly when we met, for otherwise he'd have known better than to lay a finger on anyone I cared for. That was his great mistake.

"I'm going to pay him back in his own coin. As he robbed you of something precious, so shall I take from him that which he wants with all the hunger I saw in him.

"Oh yes, my dear, I'll settle my account with him before I'm finished; you have my oath on that."

SEVEN

Lyndon held out against Arminta for just over three weeks. Away from her he discovered for the first time what it meant to have a conscience and he didn't like it. No other human being had ever meant a fig to him until the night of Broom's party.

Now he was in love, but the love was a forbidden one. It was precisely the latter fact which had made his proposed second step against the Howard family so satisfying. That pleasure had melted away in the depths of Arminta's eyes. What was left was a recognition of evil within himself.

As he expected, Ashton had ignored him. He had seen the expression on the viscount's face as he had looked down at Sapphire Grant. Rayne had believed what he, FitzMaurice, had wanted him to. Broom made no move either and then word came that Wilford and Sapphire were to be married. Lyndon knew he ought to be able to laugh at such a ludicrous match, but he couldn't. It was then that he knew he had to see Arminta again.

He didn't know why he chose the hour of eleven to arrive at Hambledon Hill. It had just seemed right to him and he felt no surprise when he saw Arminta there. She had sent Lela

Thornley for a walk, bidding her not to return for at least an hour. Lela was foolish and romantic, with no idea what real passion could do to those smitten by its power. She was sure her mistress was conducting a secret, but entirely innocent, flirtation with a young nobleman of impeccable birth. In any event, she doted on the earl's daughter and always did whatever Minty wanted her to do.

FitzMaurice walked slowly towards Arminta. In her presence he felt a different man. She melted the resentment in him and made the past a dim, half-forgotten thing. There was no awkwardness between them, or the formality of a newly-formed acquaintanceship. It was as if they'd known each other all their lives and had been reunited after a lapse of no more than a day.

"Did you think I wouldn't come? It's been three weeks or more." Lyndon was dazzled by her smile, utterly content now that he was near her.

"Oh, no. I knew you'd get here eventually and I'm a very patient person."

"I'd made up my mind not to see you again."

"But then you found you had to. You're afraid of what has happened to us, aren't you? You don't have to be, you know."

She was exquisite in her riding-habit, her hair silver-fair under the black top hat. He wanted to hold her to him and never let her go. She was all he needed; all he would ever need to sustain life.

"I suppose not. I wonder why we met."

"How funny you are." She wasn't mocking him; she merely invited him to share her laughter. "We had to meet."

"But what if I hadn't accepted Broom's invitation?"

"Then I would have found you on another occasion. It was ordained, my dearest, haven't you realised that yet?"

"Yes, I think I have. Arminta—"

"Minty."

"Minty, you don't know what sort of man I am."

"According to local gossip you are dangerous."

"And wicked, too."

"Probably. When are you going to stop talking and kiss me? You wanted to kiss me that first evening, didn't you?"

"Very much."

"I wanted you to as well. Don't you think we've wasted enough time?"

"Are you sure about this?"

"Very sure, aren't you?"

Slowly he took her in his arms, bending his head until their lips met. Minty closed her eyes in bliss. She no longer blamed her father and Ashton for keeping her in a glass case. Unknowingly, they had been saving her for Lyndon. Her whole being was vibrantly alive as she felt his body against hers, a new excitement she had never known before filling her mind.

He was so good to look at, but she knew that wasn't really important. If he'd been as plain as a flemsack she would still have yearned for him. There was something in him which touched the very core of her existence and it couldn't be ignored. It didn't matter whether he was rich or poor, good or bad, kind or cruel. Everything was irrelevant except that they had been born for the sole purpose of loving each other.

After a while they made plans for their next rendezvous. Then Lyndon said quietly:

"You know that this may not last for long?"

She was in the seventh heaven, cradled in the safety of his arms. She heard the sadness in him and was quick to console.

"Yes I know, but people worry too much about time; it's so silly. A perfect week, when one has reached the ultimate peak of joy, is worth a hundred years of ordinary living."

"I hope we shall have longer than seven days."

"I expect we will, but when the end comes we mustn't fight it or complain. Already we have been given so much. Lela will be back soon. Kiss me once more and tell me you love me."

Their mouths shared nectar, oblivious to their surroundings and the future.

"Minty." Lyndon could feel a pricking behind his eyes. It was another phenomenon with which he was unfamiliar, but he knew it had something to do with the girl he adored. "I love you so much."

"Dear, dear Lyndon, I love you, too. How very lucky we are to be blessed like this, aren't we? I wonder what we did to deserve it."

When the earl and Ashton got back they soon found out about Minty's attendance at Wilford's party.

They could never be cross with her for long and when she told them that she had gone for Sapphire's sake, they accepted her motive without further question. Both thought she looked lovelier than ever. There was a glow about her which neither had seen before. But they expected to find purity in her, and that was all they saw.

Minty was sorry she had to lie to her father and brother, just as she had regretted fooling Aunt Dorothea, who had now returned home. It couldn't be helped. Much as she cared for her family, Lyndon had to come first.

There had been more accidents in Hatley Mine in the past two weeks and the earl was grim.

"It's damned odd that things have got so much worse since FitzMaurice arrived," he said to Ashton when Minty had left the room. "I'm beginning to wonder about the man."

Rayne looked at his father and frowned.

"Just a coincidence, surely?"

"Perhaps, but he managed to get Axby by underhand means and he knew quite well I was in the course of buying it. Maybe it's more than mere coincidece."

Ashton didn't answer at once. His own hatred of Fitz-Maurice was so intense that he could barely be rational about the man. Yet even FitzMaurice would have hesitated before taking upon himself the responsiblity for the deaths of the men, women and children at Hatley. Then the viscount thought again, and wasn't so certain about that. The man was ruthless enough, that was obvious, but why was he attacking the Howards? First the colliery he had secured, well aware than the earl wanted it; now more calamities a Hatley than ever before.

Rayne dismissed his suspicions. They had probably only come into his mind because of what he had seen on that Sunday afternoon. He couldn't be objective about their new neighbour and was ready to blame him for anything which came to pass.

He felt dead inside, Sapphire's words coming back to him again and again. 'No other man will ever touch me', she had said. Yet she had lain with Lyndon FitzMaurice and, by the way she'd been screaming, had got more than she had bargained for. He longed to find an excuse for her; a reason why she had been in such an isolated spot, alone with a man.

No explanation came to him. She must have gone to the house of her own free will; FitzMaurice could scarcely have carried her there. Her professed love had been a tissue of lies. She had made a complete fool of him and he hoped he would never see her again. He didn't want to look at her beauty and dwell on the rottenness which lay beneath the surface.

He realised that his father had spoken again, and apologised for his inattentiveness. The earl noticed nothing untoward in his son; he was too busy thinking about FitzMaurice.

"I said I've been told he would like to get hold of Bluehill. So would I come to that. Perhaps he wants my pit as well. He could be trying to soften me up so that I'll be glad to get rid of the thing. Well, he won't budge me.

"Whatever happens I'll never sell Hatley to Lyndon FitzMaurice. I'll see him burn in hell first."

Essie had just commenced her journey to the pit-bottom when she heard the sound which everyone below ground dreaded more than the Devil himself. The wooden props where Tobias was working were beginning to give way. She watched them, paralysed, as the cracks widened. Then she got her voice back and shouted to Locket to move, but it was too late. The timbers split in half, bringing down part of the roof on him.

There were many hazards in the mines. Flooding, fire damp, explosion, and suffocation when the air-doors entrusted to small children didn't function properly. But, of all the disasters, a roof fall was the one which scared Essie the most. To her, there could be no worse fate than being buried alive.

Men came as fast as they could from their own section of the coal face. It was hard to hurry at the best of time; now they had to fight their way over mounds of coal and great lumps of wood, choked with dust and half-blind in the semi-darkness.

Toby was ashen under his grime, and Essie discarded her load and knelt beside him. It was her mother's story all over again and her panic was hard to conceal.

"Oh, luv, luv, what's 'appened to 'ee?"

He tried to smile, not wanting Essie to worry.

"Got me legs trapped. Can't get 'em loose."

Essie and the other miners worked like Trojans to remove the heavy debris, but it was useless. Locket was jammed tight and those about him exchanged looks of fear, for they knew what that meant.

When at last the surgeon arrived, Essie's teeth began to chatter. He was a rough, burly man, employed by several mine owners for tasks of the kind now confronting him. He drank like a fish and was incapable of feeling others' pain. He gave Locket one look and shrugged.

"I'll have to amputate; nothing else for it. His legs are too badly crushed to save anyway."

"No!" Essie blanched. "Sir, you can't, you can't!"

He barely glanced at her as he opened his bag and took out clamps, a knife and a saw.

"Either that or he dies here."

A wedge was put into Toby's mouth for him to bite on, two or three men gripping the upper part of his body at the surgeon's direction. Essie took one of his hands, whispering comfort and praying at the same time.

When she saw a gush of blood and heard Toby's frantic screams, she thought she was going to faint. Somehow she managed to keep from slumping over, still holding his hand which was now clawing convulsively. It was a mercy when Locket lost consciousness, everyone letting their breath go. Those watching had seen it all before, but they never got

112

hardened to the sight of a man's limbs being lopped off. Each of them realised it could be his turn next.

Essie waited until the next day before calling to enquire about Toby. She wasn't looking forward to meeting Mrs Locket, but she couldn't let Toby think she didn't care.

Mrs Birdie Locket was a thin woman, hair pulled tightly back until her face looked like a skull. No one knew why she was called Birdie except, as her enemies said, it was because she resembled a wizened old crow.

"What you want?"

Her hostility hit Essie like a buffet on the cheek. The small eyes pierced her flesh, the slit of a mouth issued its own warning.

"I want to see Toby."

"Well, you can't."

"But I must! He's had such a dreadful accident that I—"

Yellow teeth were bared, the grating voice full of acrimony.

"Don't you think I know that, you gormless lump? I'm 'is ma, ain't I? It's me what's got to look to 'im, changin' them bandages, moppin' up blood and pus. Me what's got to find summat to buy food wi', now 'e won't earn no more. Get away with 'ee; go on, be off."

Essie persisted but without success.

"I've 'eard 'im mention you," said Birdie as she put her hand on the door to close it. "Thinks 'e's sweet on 'ee, or did. Well, you're wastin' your time 'ere, girl. 'E won't be no use to 'ee or any other woman after this."

Essie turned away, tears in her eyes. How she was ever going to get past Toby's dragon of a ma she didn't know. But she meant to see him eventually, whatever she had to do to gain entry to the cottage. Meanwhile, there was a more pressing matter to attend to. Mrs Locket had been right about one thing. Since Toby wouldn't work again, someone had to provide food. The thought that Toby might be hungry as well as maimed gave her the courage to tramp up to Salter's Lodge and tell Sapphire what had happened.

"Essie, my dear, how awful! I'm so terribly sorry. Poor

113

Toby—he's so young."

"And 'is ma won't let me see 'im."

Sapphire, still bleeding inside from her own wounds, understood Essie's grief. If it had been Ashton lying on the mattress, stumps where his legs should have been, she would have felt just like Essie.

She gave the girl food and money and some advice.

"Leave these on the doorstep for the moment. Give Mrs Locket time to get over what's happened. She may be a horrid woman, but she is his mother. It must have been a dreadful shock to her."

Essie nodded. There was something in what Miss Sapphire was saying. She thought her former teacher looked very pale, but perhaps she merely had a headache or the usual woman's troubles. It wasn't polite to ask about private problems like that.

"I'll do what you say, Miss." Essie took the basket and money with heartfelt thanks. "But I'm goin' to see 'im in the end. I don't care if there's an army standin' at the door to stop me. I'm getting meself in one way or t'other; got no choice. I loves 'im, legs or no legs. Oh, Jesus! I love 'im so bluddy much I could die of it. 'E's got to be told that. After all, it's all 'e's got left now, ain't it?"

A week after their meeting at Hambledon Hill, Lyndon and Minty became lovers.

They had taken to walking in a small wood nearby, hidden away from the world and its prying eyes. They both knew the inevitability of their complete union. Minty hadn't been afraid of it, and his raging need for her had silenced FitzMaurice's growing doubts.

As they sat under a tree one afternoon, Minty said:

"I think it should be today, dearest."

He turned to look at her, torn between desire and an acknowledgement of his own degeneracy.

"You must be absolutely certain, Minty. It's a big step to take."

It was a far bigger step than she realised and he was trying to screw up enough courage to admit the truth when she undid the buttons down the front of her bodice.

In a few seconds she was naked to the waist and he was overcome by a fever which blotted out everything, including the baseness of the sin he was about to commit.

"Oh, my darling," he said softly. "You are so beautiful."

"I'm glad, for your sake. And I'm very sure. You said this might not last for long, and I know you're right about that. We've wasted seven days, Lyndon. Don't let's squander any more."

They came together softly at first, he half-afraid to touch her in case he bruised the pure white skin. But then she made fierce demands of which he had not thought her capable. After that, all reservation left him as he pushed her to the grass and finished undressing her.

He knew how to arouse women and Minty was eager to be set free from maidenhood. She responded with fire in her kiss, her small hands knowing instinctively how to stimulate him. She was aware of an unbearable itch which drove chastity away and made her hips writhe with carnal desires.

His hand on her breasts inflamed her; his flesh against hers drove her to the edge of frenzy. Then she felt their bodies fused together by his manhood, moaning in ecstasy as he began to satisfy the wild craving inside her. She gripped him tightly so that he should escape before his task was done, her mind and senses reeling with the wonder of what was happening.

At last it was over and they lay side by side exhausted but totally at peace.

"It was more beautiful than anything I have ever dreamed of," said Minty when she sat up and let Lyndon help her to dress. "I knew it would be perfect between us, but I didn't realise now what you could really do to me."

Lyndon kissed her, his lips hard against hers. He knew that soon he would be filled with self-recriminations because of what had taken place, but just then he only wanted to think about Minty and the precious gift she had given him.

Absorbed in the fulfilment of their love, neither noticed the man crouching down behind a clump of bushes watching them. They said goodbye, Minty as demure as ever as Lela Thornley arrived to take her home.

Smithers, the Earl of Stonehurst's chief groom, had hardly been able to believe his eyes. Like her father and brother, he had always thought of Miss Minty as a child, innocent and unsullied. Now he had witnessed her shame and with Lyndon FitzMaurice of all men.

He got back to Lindborough Hall as fast as he could, but it was two hours before the earl came home. As he listened to his groom, Stonehurst's face was bleached.

He didn't wait to see Arminta and hear her side of the story. Smithers was reliable and by now the earl was half out of his mind with fury against FitzMaurice.

He rode straight to Deerpark Manor, Smithers behind him, brushing the butler and Curle aside as he strode into the drawing-room where FitzMaurice had been doing some hard thinking.

When Lyndon had decided to commit incest, it had never occurred to him that when the time came he would be in love with his half-sister. He had wanted to change his plans for Minty's sake, but his passion for her was too strong to heed his better nature.

Through Minty's eyes he had become aware of so much to which he'd been blind before. He hadn't become a changed man overnight simply because of her. In business affairs he remained as relentless as ever, and the Yorkshire miners who had infiltrated Hatley still went about their work on his instructions. The difference was that now he could see not only himself as he really was, but had become conscious of other people in a new light. They weren't simply pieces on a chessboard for him to manipulate; they were made of flesh and blood with hopes and needs, capable of experiencing pain or happiness.

It was as if there had been a dam inside him. Never before had he recieved, or given, even mild affection, and he'd felt no lack of it. Now the floodgates had burst and he had been

116

hurtled along in a vortex of emotion which he couldn't curb.

He had got to the point of self-disgust when Stonehurst burst in on him. The earl took no notice of Curle and Smithers in the doorway as he let loose a string of scalding invective.

"I'll see you dead for this," he said, his face a mottled purple. "You're the one responsible for what's been going on in my mine, and now you've made a whore of my daughter. Why? Damn you to hell, you blackguard, why?"

Already racked with his own agony, Lyndon lost his temper. Not as the earl had done, but coldly, icily.

"Don't you really know, my lord? Look at me carefully. Note my mouth and chin—aren't they familiar? The line of my jaw is just the same as yours. Don't you remember a woman who had eyes the colour of mine? She had dark curls, I'm told, just as I had once. Her name was Flora Brown. If I'm without morals, as you are, it's because I'm your son. Your illegitimate son whom you handed over to the Greys since you wanted no part of me."

Stonehurst felt as if the floor had given way under him and there was an agonizing pain burning in his chest.

"My—my son?" he asked at last, the words tame and hollow after all the shouting. "But if that's true, Arminta's your half-sister."

"Exactly so." Lyndon's smile was cruel. "A fitting payment on account, don't you think?"

"It's incest."

Stonehurst's hand was clenched against his heart, trying to stop its unbearable throbbing.

"It's love." Lyndon said it very softly, as if he were talking to himself. "It wasn't meant to be at first, of course, but it is now. I'll never leave her alone. She's mine, and there's nothing you can do about it."

As the earl lurched out and somehow got back into the saddle, FitzMaurice hurried forward and caught Smithers' arm.

"Wait!" The command was not to be ignored and the groom made no attempt to struggle. There was death in the yellow eyes which held his own and, much as he respected the earl, he cared a good deal more for his own skin. "Here is money. It's enough for you to start up on your own. Go south now, this very minute. If you refuse, or turn back, or ever speak of what you've seen or heard, be sure I shall find you. And when I do, I shall strangle you with my own hands, do you understand?"

Smithers was on the point of collapse, but he managed to nod and give his promise. Then he was gone like a jack-rabbit and FitzMaurice ran out and made for his own mount.

He had seen the state the earl was in when the latter had left the Manor. It wasn't only rage which had made him look as he did, nor stumble like a drunken man as he walked. He was unwell, too, but exactly how ill FitzMaurice had to know. He had silenced the groom. For Minty's sake he had to make sure her father didn't talk either.

He was prepared to commit murder to save her reputation, but Dame Fortune had not turned away from him yet. Keeping out of sight as much as possible, he tracked Stonehurst's slow progress to the gates of Lindborough Hall, abandoning his horse which might betray his presence.

He shadowed the earl along the winding drive until the latter fell, lying inert. Two gardeners cried out as they threw down their tools and ran to their master. Quickly, Lyndon took cover in the thick bushes which bordered the path, creeping closer to Stonehurst. Then he saw the viscount racing from the Hall at the servant's urgent summons.

Ashton knelt by the earl's side, not able to believe what was taking place. Stonehurst was grey now, lips blue as they began to move slowly and painfully.

"Father, what is it? Dear God, I must get a physician. Bates, Darwin, fetch Dr Laughton, and hurry."

"Too—too late." The earl was making a last supreme effort, oblivious to the crowd of servants who had followed the viscount and were now clustered round him. He had something to say to his son and he knew he had no time to waste. "Ash—Ashton—save her—save her—"

No one but Lyndon FitzMaurice would have had the nerve

or assurance to take his place at the back of the anxious throng. He had calculated his chances of being spotted, weighing them against the reaction of Stonehurst's retainers. Rayne wouldn't have any eyes for him either; he was too busy listening to the earl's dying whisper.

He drew nearer still as the earl's valet said hesitatingly:

"What did he say, my lord? I couldn't catch it."

"He said 'save her, save her', but I don't know what he meant."

The words were echoed by all, even down to the kitchen-maids who had left their sinks and dishes to see what all the excitement was about.

"Save her—save her—"

They repeated it over and over again and FizMaurice smiled coldly. He wouldn't have to do away with his father after all. Stonehurst had had a heart attack, or something similar, without telling anyone about Minty. She was safe, and as quietly as a shadow he withdrew to the bushes again and then out of the grounds where he found his horse waiting.

Later, Dr Laughton confirmed heart failure.

"He was shocked." Ashton was pacing the room, great sorrow mingled with a fear he couldn't put his finger on. "I saw his face. Something had happened whilst he was out riding; something so petrifying that it killed him. I gather Smithers, his groom, went with him, but the man's nowhere to be found, so we can't question him. Perhaps he, too, was frightened and ran. If so, we shan't see him again."

Laughton nodded. He'd heard all about Stonehurst's last words; everyone was still talking about the mystery.

"You've no idea what he was trying to say?"

Ashton didn't answer at once. From the moment life had left his father's body he had had an irrational presentiment that it was Minty whom he had to save. But if that were so, why hadn't the earl spoken her name? In any event, what was there to save her from? She had been in her room, full of happiness as she and Lela arranged flowers, when he had broken the news to her.

119

All he saw in her was natural grief. There was nothing else, and his father's plea was still as much a puzzle as ever.

"No," he said at last, shaking his head at the physician's question. "I don't know what he was trying to say and now I never will. It was the last time he asked anything of me, but I was too late. Oh, Christ, Laughton, I failed him. I got there too late."

Two weeks went by and Lyndon and Minty continued to meet. He had comforted her when she had wept for her father, trying not to listen to the small inner voice which reminded him that he was responsible for Stonehurst's death. It was obvious from what Minty said that neither the new earl, nor anyone else, had guessed the truth of things. Certainly Minty herself didn't and she gave herself to him with increasing rapture.

At Salter's Lodge, Sapphire's shell was hardening. She still went down to the church each Sunday to teach, but even the tired children saw a difference in her. Her smile, when it came at all, wasn't as it used to be. She was often sharp with them when they were inattentive, and she left immediately the class was over, not stopping to chat to them as she had once done.

She did not let her resolve to protect herself spill over on to Matthew. She knew the boy loved her and she was happiest when she was with him, for then she could let her guard down.

Broom watched her sadly. She would never again be the laughing, carefree girl he had met at the vicarage. That wasn't surprising, seeing what she had been through. He still wanted to tell Ashton Howard what had really happened, but he knew Sapphire would never agree.

Sapphire didn't cheat on Wilford. She became the companion he had asked her to be, solicitous, attentive to his needs. She read to him when his eyes grew tired, showing affection and secretly worrying because Will suddenly seemed to be older and less fit.

Broom had heard about Stonehurst's death and his last words which nobody had understood. As Wilford wasn't able to go riding or walking very often, he would sit by the window in the drawing-room, wondering what the dead man had been trying to say. Clearly a woman was involved, but who?

Perhaps Stonehurst had a mistress; most men of his rank did. But it was unlikely that he would ask his son to save her, and why should she need saving anyway? His daughter, far too cosseted in Wilford's opinion, wasn't at risk, and by no stretch of the imagination could it be Sapphire of whom the dying earl had spoken.

Sapphire was getting ready for the nuptials which were to take place in the late autumn. Broom was very generous, and she protested at the number of clothes and jewels which he bought for her. The dressmaker came and made more alterations to the cream-coloured gown she was to wear on the day. Sapphire looked at her reflection in the long mirror, her heart like a stone.

Marrying Will was the only sensible course and, as he had said, she would be comfortably settled for life. Megan had expressed no surprise in her letter of congratulations. Sapphire guessed that her mother would understand her tribulation and that was why she had written lightly and without questions.

But Sapphire's wedding-day never came. Wilford fell seriously ill some weeks before, his condition worsening day by day. It hurt Sapphire to watch him struggling for breath. He was no longer round and red-cheeked, but waxen in complexion, the flesh falling off his bones.

One evening, as the light was fading, he slipped away quietly, his hand still in Sapphire's.

Sapphire wept for him, for she had loved him rather in the way she had loved her father. He had been a good man, and kindness itself when she had needed help. After the funeral, John Bourne, Broom's lawyer, explained the terms of the will.

"Apart from a trust fund to be set up for Matthew, everything goes to you. The house, the money—all of it."

Sapphire nodded, not much interested. She would rather have had Will back than his wealth.

"There is one thing, though." Bourne was turning to the last page of the document in his hand. "Mr Broom made a codicil to the will only a short time ago."

"Oh?" Even then Sapphire showed no concern. "You mean a gift to someone?"

"No, no, nothing like that. It's about Bluehill. In the original will it was to be yours without strings. Now it remains in your possession unless and until you marry."

Then Sapphire did raise her head, her attention caught at last.

"Why did he do that?"

"He didn't give me his reasons, but I suspect it was to protect you from adventurers. It's true that some men might try to win your hand simply for what you've got already, but the real money is in that mine. It will go on producing a great deal of it for many years to come. If any rogue thought to persuade you to marry him because of that, he'd be unlucky. On your marriage, Bluehill would pass to the Crown."

Something stirred at the back of Sapphire's mind, but it was too nebulous for her to see its true shape. She just remembered that Will had said FitzMaurice would never acquire his colliery. Now she knew Broom had taken steps to see that neither Lyndon, nor anyone else, could do so by using her as a pawn. She wondered whether Will had taken the precaution before or after she had been raped. She didn't ask Bourne when the new clause had been added; it really didn't matter. She dismissed her fleeting thoughts as of no consequence. FitzMaurice wouldn't want to marry her. Men never wed the women they violated, or so she had been assured by Megan when the latter was warning her about the dangers of predators.

"Yes, I see. And if I don't marry?"

"Then, of course, the colliery remains yours and you draw the royalties."

"No one knows of this codicial but you and me, do they?"

The lawyer looked mildly scandalized by such a question.

"Of course not, Miss Grant. You, my confidential clerk, and myself are the only three privy to that information."

A brief smile touched Sapphire's lips. It was sour, no

humour in it. What a joke it would be if some avaricious fortune-hunter did coax her to marry him, just to lay hands on the mine. On their wedding-night she would be able to present him with a copy of the codicil and enjoy the blank consternation on his face. For no reason at all the thought of FitzMaurice came into her head again, and she gave a small shiver.

"Thank you, sir," she said, quickly pushing Lyndon out of her mind. "You've been most kind and helpful. Now, what about a nice cup of tea before you leave?"

EIGHT

Stonehurst was scarcely cold in his grave before two more catastrophes occurred at Hatley.

The new earl knew then that he had to find out what was going on before any more lives were lost, and questioned some of the miners as they came off their shifts. They assured him that they'd seen no one doing anything below ground which he shouldn't have been doing, adding a few colourful promises as to what would happen to such a man if found.

Something prompted Ashton to ask if they had known anyone else called FitzMaurice; a family which, perhaps, had moved away some years ago. Again they shook their heads, George Greenhalgh acting as their spokesman.

"Nay, m'lord. Weren't no one o' that name till gentleman at Deerpark Manor arrived."

"Was there any other family who left the area?"

Greenhalgh scratched his head.

"Don't think so. Born 'ere, die 'ere, that's us. Eh, wait a minute though. There were the Greys, o' course. They 'ad a funny lad with a mop of black curls. Thought 'imself a cut above everybody else, and ran off one night wi'out a word. 'Is name were Donald and 'e were as queer as Dick's hatband to be sure."

"How old was he?"

George shrugged.

"Never asked. 'Bout eighteen or so, wouldn't you reckon?"

The rest murmured their agreement, but Ashton wasn't yet satisfied.

"When did he go?"

"Gawd luv us, m'lord, can't tell 'ee that. Mebbe six or seven summers back. Long afore 'is folk did, at any rate."

The earl was pensive, but it wasn't enough to go on and FitzMaurice certainly didn't have black curls. Then he went to St Luke's to talk to the Reverend Cecil Hornby. At the earl's request the incumbent searched the registers for the past twenty-five years, but stated regretfully that there wasn't a single entry concerning a family of the name in question.

It was while the vicar was putting the books away that Ashton happened to glance up at a stone plaque, nibbled away by age. The carved inscription seemed to leap out of the wall at him and he gave a slight exclamation.

"My lord?" Mr Hornby hurried to his side. "Is anything wrong?"

"No, but this parish had one FitzMaurice at least, but I doubt if the owner of the Manor had such illustrious ancestors. I doubt it very much indeed."

Ashton left the vestry, his frown deeper than ever. Another coincidence? It was almost too much of one, but if it wasn't that, what else could it possibly be?

Sapphire went into the velvet drawing-room, her fingers moving lightly over the articles on the desk, just as they had done when she was a child.

Mrs Sheldon had been so sad because she couldn't give her young visitor the house of her dreams. Now, thanks to Will, Sapphire was mistress of Salter's Lodge and all the treasures it contained.

It ought to have given her complete satisfaction, but it didn't.

125

Every day as she wandered from room to room her thoughts were of Ashton and the look on his face when he had turned away from her cry for help. She nursed a brooding resentment against the man who had raped her, but some anger for Ashton, too. He had jumped to a conclusion without waiting to hear the facts. He had been judge, jury and executioner, and it was hard to forgive him for that.

Yet, in spite of her sense of injustice, it was really the rest of the time they had spent together which brought her close to tears. She missed his arms about her, his mouth compelling submission of her own.

When Rose, her parlourmaid, came to tell her that Mr FitzMaurice had called to see her, she nodded. The girl who had struggled frantically on the bed in the corner of a darkened room wouldn't have been able to face him. The poised young woman, whose heart was frozen, felt more than a match for her seducer and received him as if they were merely casual acquaintances.

FitzMaurice gave a brief bow and went straight to the point.

"You must think it outrageous of me to come here like this, but I had to tell you that I'm sorry for what I did. My words aren't just idle apologies. I mean it; I bitterly regret my abominable behaviour."

As Sapphire gestured to Lyndon to sit down, she could see that he was telling the truth. It was a surprise; she hadn't expected him to give the episode another thought. However, she wasn't going to let him off that easily no matter how real his remorse was.

"No doubt you do, sir, but not as much as I."

"Naturally. You were the one who was injured. I wish I could make you believe me. If there was only something I could do."

Her smile was derisive.

"It's rather difficult to turn a prostitute into a virgin again."

"You weren't a prostitute; never think that of yourself. All the blame was mine."

"Perhaps not all. I was unwise to be so trusting. I had been told you weren't kind, yet I allowed myself to believe you wanted to help those children."

"It was a moment of madness."

"No, it wasn't. That regretable incident had been carefully planned. The strange thing is that I knew from the moment you touched me that you didn't want me as a woman. You derived no pleasure from me, did you?"

He was startled; she was much more percipient than he'd realised.

"You've grown up, haven't you?"

"Yes, girlhood doesn't last long in such circumstances. Well, are you going to tell me what it was all about?"

She saw his expression change, but didn't understand it, listening to his further self-abasement and wondering what was really going on in his mind.

"—and so it must remain as madness. Have I a hope of pardon?"

Sapphire thought of the dingy room once more, and then of Ashton, and shrugged.

"It's over now; finished. Yes, I'll accept your apology."

He was about to thank her for her generosity when she said coolly: "And what of the other matter you've come to see me about? I'm sure there is another reason for this visit."

"You have become too astute for me."

"That I doubt. Men of mean intelligence don't succeed as you have done. No, Mr FitzMaurice, in most things you would leave me far behind, but I know what you want. It's Bluehill, isn't it?"

"You take my breath away. But, as you don't bandy words, neither will I. Yes, I want it."

"So I'm sure does the Earl of Stonehurst."

That time she had no difficulty at all in reading the look in the tawny eyes. It was pure, unadulterated hatred and she felt a thrill of fear run through her. Hurt though she'd been by Ashton, her natural instinct was to protect him. She hadn't realised that he and FitzMaurice even knew each other; Ashton always chose his friends with great care. Yet for a second or two her guest had had murder written on his face. Such a patent enmity couldn't have been aroused by a total stranger.

To turn FitzMaurice away would be unwise. She needed to watch him and try to assess the reason for his feelings and what he was going to do about them.

Lyndon had regained complete self-control, doubting if Sapphire Grant had noticed his momentary lapse. She looked placid enough, but he would have to be more careful in future. She had given ample evidence that she was nobody's fool.

"Yes, I suppose he will approach you. Still, you may find my proposition will be of great interest to you. Perhaps it is inappropriate to discuss details today. I find that humble pie doesn't mix with business. May I call on you again?"

"Of course." Sapphire was glad that the suggestion had come from him, for she didn't want to know how closely she proposed to observe him from then on. "I shall be happy to see you at any time."

"Then I will send you a note. Meanwhile, you will think over my suggestion of buying your colliery, won't you?"

Her smile was without guile.

"Certainly, Mr FitzMaurice. Indeed, I doubt if I shall think about anything else until we next meet. I will have to sharpen up my wits and you, in turn, sir, be warned. I have already been tricked by you and I don't intend to let it happen again. Once was quite enough for me."

After another three visits from FitzMaurice, during which Sapphire had kept him dangling on a string, her maid came to announce that the Earl of Stonehurst was asking to see her.

She longed to remain as calm and collected as she'd been when FitzMaurice had called, but the very mention of Ashton's name made her pulse jump. She took a deep breath, forcing herself to stillness as she told Rose to show him in.

At first, she had found it odd to think of Ashton as the Earl of Stonehurst. Now she had grown used to it. In time she would have to learn to accept a new Viscount Rayne, when Allene gave Ashton a son.

As he crossed the room it took all her will-power to stop herself from holding her arms out to him. His face was so dear to her; his tall, elegant body made her shake with something other than fear.

It was the same for Ashton. As he got close to Sapphire, his heart contracted. He had never known a woman with eyes like hers, nor a mouth so perfectly designed for his kiss.

Sapphire pulled herself together. If she could deal with FitzMaurice, she should be able to deal with this severe critic of hers.

"My lord? This is an unexpected—pleasure."

He cringed inwardly at the mockery in her voice. It wasn't part of the Sapphire he still wanted as much as ever and his response was tart.

"Perhaps you mean intrusion. Let me assure you that I have come to discuss a matter of business and have no intention of staying for long."

"How desolate you make me feel." Sapphire thought she was keeping her end up very well, but she didn't like the lump in her throat, nor the smarting behind her eyelids. "Please do sit down, if only for a moment."

"Thank you. Now, what I have come to ask is—"

"—whether I will sell Bluehill to you."

He looked exactly the same as on the day Allene Telford had made a gaffe about Decimus's lack of money. He had frightened her then and it was no different now.

"You must be gifted with second-sight, madam."

"Not at all. You would hardly come to see me as a—a friend."

He heard the faint quaver, but by now he was as frosty as she had been.

"Hardly . I'm told FitzMaurice has called on you several times."

"What an excellent intelligence service you have. But you must have assumed he would do so. You made other assumptions quickly enough."

"May we please stop discussing something which I, at any rate, would prefer to forget."

The tears were getting closer and she clenched her hands behind the folds of her dress where Ashton couldn't see them.

"I have no wish to dwell on that occasion either. Let us by all means turns to the reason for your presence here. Mr FitzMaurice has offered me a very good price. If I go on coaxing him I'm sure I can get more from him."

"I don't doubt it."

"Then you'll have to bid against him, won't you?"

"Damn it, Sapphire, why are you doing this? You must have forgotten what it's like down a mine if you can even contemplate selling to FitzMaurice. Elstone is a scandal, and you know it."

Her lips tightened. Ashton was judging her again, this time implying that she had no thought for the workers at Bluehill.

"I don't know it," she replied bleakly. "I have only seen the vile conditions in Hatley Mine and that, my lord, belongs to you." She knew his temper was rising, but she didn't care any more. "Perhaps you'll be more fortunate in your quest than your father was over Axby. He didn't move nearly fast enough there, did he?"

Ashton got to his feet, his blood boiling.

"You damned trollop! When I saw you with FitzMaurice I was appalled. Later, I tried to find excuses for you, but there were none. I was right about you. You took your pleasure where you wanted and then managed to get Broom to offer marriage so you could get your greedy hands on his money. He was old enough to be your father."

"How dare you talk to me like that, you insufferable prig? You know nothing about what happened on that Sunday afternoon, because you didn't care enough about me to stop and ask. You didn't want to bother with an impecunious parson's daughter. Oh yes, you kissed me and told me that you loved me, but only because you were bored and couldn't find anyone else with whom to make sport. Damn you, damn you, get out of here!"

130

"You don't know what you're saying. I did love you; I truly did. But you snuffed out that love most efficiently when you stripped yourself naked for FitzMaurince. I hope he paid you well."

"I didn't strip myself. Don't exaggerate. You saw him tear my dress from me, and he didn't pay me a penny."

"My commiserations. Here—" He threw four guineas on to the carpet in front of her. "I have taken up your valuable time when you could have been earning this elsewhere."

As he flung himself on to his horse, Ashton felt as if his world was coming to an end. It had been torture to be so near to Sapphire and not be able to touch her. He had told her that he had once loved her, but the lie concerning his present feelings had to be sustained.

Now he could never bring himself to admit that he still worshipped her and, worse, that he would go on doing so until the day he died.

Essie Gosling waited until Mrs Locket had emerged from her cottage and shuffled off down the cobbled street before she climbed in through one of the windows. It wasn't easy, because of her bad leg and the parcel she was carrying, but her will was like tempered steel.

She hadn't been able to go on working at Hatley after Toby's accident. Making trips to the spot where she'd seen him, first half-buried and then mutilated with a knife and saw, had proved too much for her. She didn't particularly want to work for Mr FitzMaurice, bearing in mind his reputation, but Elstone was fairly near to her home and there had been a vacancy.

Tobias, huddled on his mattress in a slough of despondency, thought he was dreaming. His mother had told him Essie hadn't been near nor by, and it hadn't occurred to him that she might have been lying.

He looked at Essie's funny snub nose and wide smile, the pale green eyes shining for him, and wanted to weep. But she must have come out of pity, and he didn't want any of that.

131

Even if there were some other reason, he loved her too much to condemn her to the sort of life she would have with him.

"What you doin' 'ere?" he asked brusquely.

"Come to see you, of course, what else?"

"No need o' that. Since you ain't been before, what's the sense of comin' now?"

Her smile faded.

"I've been 'ere afore. Came day after you was 'urt, and tried times enough after that to git in but yer ma wouldn't let me pass t'door. Didn't you 'ear us arguin'?"

"No, I sleeps a lot."

He was holding his breath, longing to feel her close to him, yet knowing he hadn't the right to ruin her life.

"Don't blame you. 'Ow are you?"

" 'Ow do you think?"

"I'm that sorry, luv. I cried buckets over you when the surgeon—that is—when—"

"When 'e chopped me legs off. No need to be afeared to say it. No secret, is it? Come to look at what's left, 'ave you?"

Essie understood his impotent rage and frustration and let the harsh words slide over her.

"No, that ain't why I've come."

"Then what?"

"To tell you I love you and that as soon as I can save up enough, we're goin' to be married."

He stared at her, desperately wanting what she was offering him. His mother had done nothing but nag him and remind him how useless he was. She hadn't told him the truth about Essie either. He needed Essie's arms round him to comfort him, but he wasn't the one who mattered.

"You're mad, girl. Like one of 'em crazed people shut up in a bedlam. Married! We couldn't 'ave wed when I was whole, much less now. 'Sides, didn't you know? It weren't only me legs I lost. Got other injuries as well. I won't never satisfy a woman again."

Essie hadn't realised Toby had suffered another blow, but the expression on her face didn't change, nor did her

132

intentions.

"Again, is it? You saucy devil. You never told me about any other wenches when we was courtin'."

"We weren't courtin'."

" 'Course we was. People don't plan weddin's and 'ow they're goin' to furnish their cottage if they ain't serious about each other."

"That's all over."

"Needn't be. Crazed I might be, but I loves you, Toby. Perhaps more 'un ever now. Let's 'old 'ands for a bit, like we used to do."

As she drew nearer he half-stretched out one hand, snatching it back at the last minute.

"No, you're only sorry for me."

"Sure I am, but that weren't why I came. And I want a kiss or two off you afore I go."

He was weakening. He hungered for her so much because she could put some hope and happiness into his empty life. The trouble was that she'd have to pay such a high price if he gave it. He was about to snap at her again when Mrs Locket returned and began to shriek at Essie.

"You bluddy 'arpy, git out o' 'ere. Didn't I tell you to stay away? What you botherin' wi' 'im for, any road? 'E can't be an 'usband to you now, nor any other bitches either. You're upsettin' 'im, remindin' 'im o' the things 'e can't 'ave. Git away wi' you, git away."

Birdie picked up a stick and began to hit Essie. It was then that Toby took on his mother for the first time since he'd been brought home lying on an old door.

"Stop that, Ma, or I'll crawl out o' 'ere and give you a few whacks meself. Leave 'er alone, can't you? If she wants to come now and then to look at a freak, let 'er."

Mrs Locket's jaw dropped. Tobias had never spoken to her like that before and this thunderous frown made her quite nervous, immobile though he was.

"That's right, Missus." Essie was rubbing her bruises. "You keep yer 'ands to yerself or I'll break yer broom over yer 'ead.

133

Toby, I'll come as often as I can. 'Ere, I've got a few bits and pieces for you. Most come from Miss Grant, but I bought the baccy meself. Thought you'd like that."

As she bent over to give him the package their eyes met. For a few seconds Essie saw the truth in him and her heart started to sing. He still felt the same; he just didn't want to saddle her with his troubles. He'd probably be rough of tongue next time she came; it was his way of protecting her from the burden he thought he'd be to her.

She straightened up and gave his mother a hard look.

"I came in by t'window, but I'm goin' out by t'door, like a Christian. You see 'e eats them victuals, or you and me are goin' to fall out reel bad and you won't like it. 'Ear me? You'll be reet sorry, Birdie Locket, and that's a promise."

As October freshened the wind and covered the ground with a carpet of burnished gold, copper, faded green and yellow, Lyndon and Minty began to meet in a disused chapel on the far side of the wood.

Lela Thornley was as naïve as ever. She still clung to her belief that Arminta was meeting a chivalrous, upright beau, and was quite content to wander about for an hour or so to give the young lovers some privacy.

One particular day, Lyndon watched Minty as she walked down the dusty aisle. She wore russet-coloured satin, trimmed with chinchilla, and carried a small muff to match. Her velvet hat piled high with ribbons was an absurdity, but he thought he'd never seen her look more beautiful.

It was while she was greeting him with a kiss that he made the final decision to break with her.

He had been thinking about it for quite a while. Luck had been with them so far, but it wouldn't favour them for ever. One day they would be caught and then Minty would be ruined. Such scandal would be bad enough, but his real fear was that Minty would find out the truth about their relationship.

He had intended to return to London until Sapphire Grant

told him the Earl of Stonehurst wanted to buy Bluehill. His hatred of the Howards hadn't diminished. The old earl was dead, and Minty was blameless. That left Ashton to pay for what his father had done and FitzMaurice had no intention of letting the earl beat him over the acquisition of Broom's colliery. In the last few days, Bluehill had become a kind of symbol to FitzMaurice. To win the mine would be to score over the Howards, rubbing the family's nose in defeat.

In any event, wherever he went Minty might follow him. It needed more than a separation to end their *affaire*. Distance might not deter Minty, but a wife most certainly would.

It had always been part of his plan to marry and have sons to carry on his name. He wanted to found a dynasty as rich and successful as those of the local aristocrats who wanted nothing to do with him. If he could persuade Sapphire Grant to marry him she would not only be a suitable wife but would also bring a satisfying dowry with her.

Curle had cultivated a warm friendship with Rose, Sapphire's parlourmaid. She had told him all about her mistress's quarrel with the earl, but there had been more to it than that.

When Rose had taken the tea-tray in a few minutes after his lordship had stormed out, Sapphire had been standing by the window, her back turned.

"She were cryin' reel hard," Rose had said to Stanley as they had taken an evening stroll. "And she said right out loud: 'Oh, Ashton, Ashton, can't you see how much I love you?' When she 'eard me, she went to 'er chair calm as you please, just as if nothin' 'ad 'appened."

Lyndon had a sixth sense about Sapphire and Ashton Howard, perhaps because he was in love himself. In spite of the violent words the earl had used, and the fact that he believed Sapphire a harlot, Lyndon thought it very likely that Ashton returned her feelings.

There could be no question of marriage between them; Ashton was already betrothed to another woman and he and Sapphire were of a different caste. Nevertheless, he wouldn't like it if Sapphire wed the man he believed to be her lover.

It made up his mind for him. He and Sapphire had been getting on quite well of late. She still kept him guessing about Bluehill, and she certainly wasn't in love with him. Yet she was too sensible to let herself become an unwanted old maid. She would realise she had to make a life of her own and he, Lyndon, would help her. She would make an excellent mother for his children and whe would get the woman he was sure Howard loved, plus the mine for which he wouldn't have to pay a penny.

He decided to say nothing to Minty until his betrothal was publicly announced. If Sapphire turned him down flat, Minty wouldn't have been hurt for nothing. If his proposal was accepted, it would be too late for Minty to try to change his mind.

It was cruel, but it had to be done. For some reason the gods had lent him this delicate, fragile creature, but they had meant him to do more than enjoy her. She was in his care and it was up to him to protect her, whatever sacrifices had to be made.

Sapphire was feeling very low when Lyndon called on her the next afternoon. She had met Ashton when she had been out walking that morning and he had cut her dead. It had been more devastating than if he had struck her across the face with his riding-whip. Then Rose told her that she'd heard Lord Telford's daughter was about to return to England.

It wasn't true, but neither Rose nor Sapphire knew that. Curle had just dropped the information casually, and Rose had lapped it up.

Sapphire wasn't really surprised when Lyndon asked her to marry him. He had been such a regular caller and she had wondered whether he had something like that on his mind. Knowing nothing of his love and anxiety for Arminta, she had assumed his main reason for asking for her hand was to gain Bluehill.

She'd given the possibility of such a move on his part much thought. Although Ashton and Allene would probably spend most of their time in London, they would undoubtedly return to Lindborough Hall for part of each year. She didn't want to sell Salter's Lodge; it meant too much to her. Equally unpalatable would be living not far from Ashton, with nothing else to do but picture him in bed with his wife.

What she needed was a busy life of her own. She loved children and wanted a full nursery. It would also be a great advantage to have a man to deal with the various enterprises which Broom had left her.

Lyndon had already done the worst thing he could ever do to her, and of late he had seemed different. It wasn't only his civility; that was to be expected. She had seen a definite change in him. He was softer and sometimes, when he thought she wasn't looking, his expression was sad. She had found him easy to talk to and his sense of humour had surprised her.

She still intended to make him pay for his attack on her, but their wedding night would take care of that. Apart from her triumph in the matter of Bluehill, Lyndon was good-looking, so her babies would be fair of face and strong of body. He was very astute and she could forget business problems. He would be good for Matthew, now at boarding-school.

She knew FitzMaurice's request had brought her to a major turning point in her life and a bold decision had to be made there and then.

She could spend many lonely years mourning for a man who didn't love her, or she could create a new world for herself. She took a deep breath.

"Yes, I'll marry you," she said lightly. "I think we will deal well enough together. You aren't in love with me, nor I with you, so there will be no heartbreak. We'll have the sons and daughters we both want. It will be a comfortable companionship of mutual support and perhaps, later, of affection."

For a second there was something in her voice which Lyndon didn't like, but the dark eyes were giving nothing away and she was right. There would be no heartbreak with her.

"I'm a lucky man," he said dryly. "As you say, it will be a pleasant existence for both of us. I'm honoured that you have accepted me, for you have beauty, brains, and courage, too."

"I also understand you, sir, and that is the most important thing of all from my point of view."

He smiled, acknowledging the dig.

"Yes, you do, don't you? I'll call on you tomorrow, if I may. We can discuss plans then."

"Just like a business partnership."

"A trifle tart, madam. Are you having second thoughts so soon?"

"Not at all. I'm just a realist, as you are. Goodbye, Lyndon, and don't waste your money buying expensive jewellery for me. I already have caskets full of it upstairs."

That time his laugh was one of genuine amusement.

"I may not be in love with you, but the more I see of you the more I like you. I'll bring you red roses instead."

When he had gone she lay back in her chair, talking silently to Broom and trying to explain things to him.

Will, you are about to get your own way. We're going to pay Lyndon FitzMaurice back in his own coin, just as you wanted to. I don't particularly relish the idea of sharing his bed, but it'll be worth it to see his face when I tell him about the codicil.

Besides, now that you're gone what else is left for me? I'll never get Ashton's love back and if I can't have that I don't much care what happens to me.

He was my *raison d'être*. But I've lost him. I'm lonely, too, and at least Lyndon is the devil I know. He has changed for the better, although I can't imagine why. I think he'll look after me and you'd want that, wouldn't you? The years soon pass and when I'm near to the grave I know I'll see you again and that's one thing which will be well worth waiting for.

Oh, my dear, kind Will, what wouldn't I give to have you back with me again.

NINE

Ashton was just about to ride away from Hatley when he saw FitzMaurice approaching him.

There had been yet another tragedy; ten dead and nine injured. One had been a child of about five and the earl had felt sick as he looked at what remained of the boy.

When Lyndon dismounted the earl frowned. He had only seen FitzMaurice once before and then for the briefest of moments. He hadn't quite realised how comely the man was. His eyes were like jewels and white hair on one of his age was unusual as well. All in all, Lyndon FitzMaurice was very attractive indeed.

"Good morning, my lord. More trouble?"

"Yes. May I ask what you're doing here?"

"I came to see you. I was told you'd set out for Hatley. My name's FitzMaurice, but I expect you know that. It's about this mine that I wanted to talk to you."

Ashton's horse was restive, forcing him to slide from the saddle. He had no desire to converse with the man who had lain with Sapphire, but he could hardly walk away without betraying his feelings.

"What about it?"

There was a shadow of a smile on Lyndon's lips.

"So many accidents of late; what a worry it must be to you. I'm sure you'd like to get rid of the thing. I'm willing to make you a generous offer for it."

"I don't wish to sell."

"I'd think it over if I were you. The loss of all those lives must distress you."

"It does, but Hatley still isn't for sale."

"Let me know if you change your mind. Oh, by the way, Miss Grant has done me the honour of agreeing to become my wife. We don't want anyone else to know about it until we are ready to make a proper announcement. But I know you're an old friend of hers and that you can be trusted to keep the news to yourself for the time being."

Ashton felt as though FitzMaurice had clubbed him over the head. He knew quite well why Lyndon wanted to marry Sapphire; it was to get her properties, including Bluehill. He had no affection for her at all, of that the earl was sure. As to why Sapphire had agreed, he could only assume that his own quarrel with her had helped in the making of her reckless decision.

He kept his face blank, not giving FitzMaurice the pleasure of seeing his reaction.

"My felicitations, sir, and I shan't tell a soul if that is your wish."

"Thank you for your good wishes and for your own discretion. Are you sure I can't persuade you to part with the mine?"

"Quite. I shall continue to shoulder my own responsibilities as I've always done."

"You're a brave man."

"Not particularly; just a stubborn one."

When they parted, Ashton began to sift the various small pieces of puzzle which were cluttering up his mind. He wished he knew what had disturbed his father to such an extent that it had brought on a heart attack. The earl's last words still defied

140

explanation. Ashton was no nearer to guessing the identity of the woman in question, or why she needed help.

There was also his father's anger over Axby and his contention that the accidents at Hatley had grown more numerous since FitzMaurice's arrival. Once, Ashton had believed the latter was a mere coincidence, but his doubts on that score were increasing.

The thought of Donald Grey, who had run away from home, continued to bother him. So did the plaque in St Luke's vestry, dedicated to a man long dead, but none of the segments would come together to make sense.

However, of one thing he was quite certain. He had to stop Sapphire from marrying FitzMaurice. It wasn't just selfishness because he loved her so desperately. It was for her own safety.

Seeing Lyndon again had made him agree with the concensus of opinion abroad at the time FitzMaurice had moved into Deerpark Manor.

Clever he might be, handsome he certainly was, but above all he was dangerous. That was something which Sapphire had to be made to see before it was too late and Ashton turned his horse's head and galloped off in the direction of Salter's Lodge.

"You can't marry him. Sapphire, you can't."

Sapphire hadn't wanted to see Ashton again, but he had stalked into the morning-room before Rose could stop him. She had been shaken to discover that he knew about the forthcoming marriage. Lyndon had asked her not to speak of it for a while. She hadn't understood his request, but she had agreed. It hadn't bothered her one way or the other, but for some reason FitzMaurice had told the earl and now the latter was there, grim-faced, his voice extremely terse.

"I shall marry whom I please, my lord. It is none of your business."

"I intend to make it mine."

"I should be grateful if you would stop interfering and go away."

141

"Not until I have your word that you'll tell FitzMaurice you've changed your mind."

"But I haven't changed it."

"Then do so now."

"I won't. You don't care a button for me. All that bothers you is the fact that Lyndon will get Bluehill and you won't. I told you you'd have to bid against him, didn't I? Well, you dragged your feet, just like your father did, and you've lost. Take your childish temper and chagrin out of here. He's won."

"Damn you, you whore."

Ashton slapped her across the face, seeing red at her intransigence and spiteful jibe.

Sapphire raised her arm to return the blow, but then the earl's fingers closed round her wrist like a vice.

A moment later they were in each other's arms, their lips healing harsh words and harsher actions.

"I never stopped loving you." Ashton took her face between his hands as he'd done so often before. "Even after that dreadful day when I saw you with FitzMaurice and you were—"

"I had just been raped."

Stonehurst's colour drained away and his limbs felt weak.

"Raped?"

"Yes. I cried out to you, but—"

"—I rode away. Dearest, come and sit down and tell me about it."

She did so, in tears by the time she'd finished, and glad of Ashton's broad shoulder to bury her head against.

"Christ! What a fool I was. I should have realised it for myself."

"I expect it did look bad."

"Yes, but I ought to have trusted you."

"I wish you had. My marriage to Lyndon is one of convenience, but I adored you."

"Adored? You no longer feel the same?"

She sat up and wiped her eyes.

"Unfortunately, I do. I wish I could get over you, because it's

142

like having an illness for which there's no cure."

"It's been the same for me for a long time. All my waking hours are filled with thoughts of you, but I could see no way of making you mine. The pain's awful, isn't it?"

"Quite terrible."

"Must you marry Lyndon?"

"Must you marry Allene?"

After a moment or two's silence he took the plunge.

"Would your servants notice if we went upstairs?"

She was holding his hand very tightly.

"I don't suppose so. Their work on the first floor is finished until this evening."

"Then let's go to your room. It may be the one and only chance we have and I need you, sweetheart. My body aches because of my hunger for you. Must I starve?"

"No." Her eyes were like stars. "I won't let that happen because I am starving, too. Just let me make sure that no one's about."

She locked the bedroom door, her heart racing. She had thought about this moment so often. Many times she had pictured the scene, altering a detail here, another there. But the end never varied. When all the words had been said, she would become his. Along with her other memories, the wonder of their intercourse would be with her for ever.

She let him undress her, the rising excitement in her turning her cheeks a deeper pink. His hands were thin and strong, but gentle where Lyndon's had been rough. She shivered as he stroked her flesh with experienced fingers, almost crying out to him to hurry as he caressed one breast, lingering over its sweet softness.

She wanted more than that from him and held him closer to her as they exchanged a kiss which bruised her lips. He pushed her down on the bed, as impatient as she was of the preliminaries.

His body felt wonderful against her own, as she'd known it would. It was hard and muscular, dominating hers with its demands. She wasn't passive herself. Her limbs entwined with

143

his as ardour began to grow to fever-pitch.

When Lyndon had raped her, the only thing she had felt was repugnance. Now it was so different. She understood for the first time what had lain dormant in the secret parts of her. The sexual urge grew fiercer as their tongues explored each other's mouths and hands found erogenous areas which heightened lust.

Her head was swimming, all sense of time and place lost as they grew nearer to a consummation of their love. She was vaguely aware that he had forced her legs apart, gasping as she reached her climax.

Then, quite suddenly, Ashton pulled away from her and she felt the shock run through her as if he had struck her again. She tried to hold on to him, begging him not to leave her. So deeply was she aroused that she almost whimpered as he stood up and started to put his clothes on.

She watched him numbly, her whole being trembling and tortured because she was unfulfilled, tears running down her cheeks when she could see his decision was final.

As he sat on the side of the bed she said shakily: "Why, Ashton, why? You don't know what you've done to me."

His face was full of pain as he held her against him.

"But I do, my darling, I do. I know exactly what I've done."

"Then why—?"

"Because if I had gone on I would be no better than FitzMaurice."

"That's not true. He took me against my will; I wanted you. Oh God, Ashton, I wanted you!"

"Oh, my dear, my dear." He rocked her back and forth, feeling the violence of her sobs and wanting to cry with her. "Forgive me, please forgive me. You are the most precious thing in the world to me. I thought I could go to bed with you and it wouldn't matter, but it does. I won't make a strumpet out of you."

She managed to look up and she saw her bleak misery, a stark reflection of his own.

"Now even if I want you to?"

144

"Not even then."

"You'd better go."

"Yes." He sighed as he rose and straightened his coat. "I've done so much harm already that you're right to send me packing. Sapphire, don't marry FitzMaurice. It's not jealousy on my part which makes me beg you to give up the idea. I don't trust him and he could hurt you terribly."

She pulled the sheet around her and said sadly: "No, he won't be able to do that because I feel nothing for him. It's you who've hurt me, Ashton, because I love you. If you had finished what you started, I think I could have faced anything which came in the future. Now that you've shewn me what being a woman means, and how savage rejection can be, I'm not sure of myself any more."

"I deserved that." He didn't know how he had managed to control himself a few minutes earlier, nor could he think how to comfort her as he left, but he tried. "It wasn't through lack of desire. You are the most beautiful and exciting woman I have ever known. My punishment will be that for the rest of my years I shall have to live with the knowledge that I could have had you. I will bear that punishment willingly because I've done you a lesser wrong by holding back."

When he had gone Sapphire got out of bed and looked at herself in the mirror. She wasn't sure whether she would ever get over her experience and certainly Lyndon wouldn't be able to satisfy the craving which Ashton had awoken in her.

As she fastened her dress she tried to hate him for what he'd done, but she couldn't. Ashton had been right, of course, and she should never have agreed to take him to her bedroom. To be forced into coition by the superior strength of a lecher was one thing; to give oneself freely and eagerly was quite another. Only harlots did that.

She smoothed her hair, trying to compose herself. She knew she would cry again that night and probably for many nights to come. She had prayed that she might belong to Ashton just once, but now she never would.

That being so, there was no reason why she shouldn't marry

Lyndon FitzMaurice, whatever the earl thought of him.

After today, nothing mattered any more.

When Minty went to tea with Sapphire and was told the latter was to marry Lyndon, she remained wholly untroubled and serene. She didn't need Sapphire to tell her the proposed match was one of convenience; she knew that already.

Lyndon had been avoiding her lately. Twice he had sent notes saying he couldn't be at the chapel at the appointed time and now she understood why.

It had puzzled her, but not because she doubted his love. He must have had very strong reasons for seeking Sapphire's hand and she mourned for him because she knew how unhappy he must be.

With Lela's help she waylaid FitzMaurice as he was riding out from Deerpark Manor. Miss Thornley obligingly made herself scarce before he appeared, still sighing sentimentally over her mistress's trysts.

Lyndon wished he could have raced straight past Minty, but that wasn't possible. He had prayed he wouldn't have to face her yet, but now he had no choice. He dismounted, looking at her with troubled eyes.

He had to tell her about Sapphire and hoped that she wouldn't break down and weep. His fears were quickly allayed as Minty reached up to kiss him.

"Don't look like that, my darling, it's all right. I know; Sapphire told me."

"She shouldn't have done so. I asked her not to."

"You mustn't be cross with her because of that. We are very close friends and you can't keep in a secret for ever."

"I have no idea how to explain this to you. Minty, it must seem that I—"

Her smile blessed him and as he saw the depths of love in her he caught her in his arms.

"Shall we go into the wood? You're not cold, are you?"

"I'm never cold when I'm with you. Yes, I'd like to go to the place where we first sat on that fallen tree trunk. Do you remember?"

"I remember everything we have done together."

"How sweet you are, Lyndon."

"That is the last thing I am. I told you once that I was wicked. You didn't believe me."

She laughed and, as always, the sound enchanted him.

"I believed you, truly I did. It was just that it made no difference to my longing for you."

When they reached the clearing she said gently: "Come and sit beside me. It will be easy now."

"I don't think it will, but I'll try. First, though, I want you to know that you are the only woman in the world whom I love. I won't insult your intelligence by pretending that I didn't have mistresses before we met. I did, but they meant nothing to me. You are the one I care for."

"I know that. I knew it from the first second we met."

He closed his eyes briefly, shutting out the vision of Minty in her yellow silk. That had been their beginning; now they were reaching their end.

"I have done you a great wrong, much greater than you know. Marriage is an impossibility for us and so I must set you free. This is the way I have chosen to do it. I thought if I simply went away you might follow me. I couldn't let that happen, so I'm going to put a lawful, wedded wife between us. That is a barrier through which neither of us can break."

She laid one hand on his cheek, gazing at him in a way which made him weak.

"I'll wait for you Lyndon."

He forced himself to be curt.

"No, you mustn't do anything so absurd. Minty, it's over."

"Not yet, not like this." Her voice was low and completely assured. "One day it will finish, but in quite a different way."

"You're talking nonsense, as if you could see into the future."

"Perhaps I can. You didn't know I was a witch, did you?"

"Don't joke about this. It's so very hard for me."

"It doesn't have to be. Marrying Sapphire won't alter things

147

between you and me. How could it? We are part of each other."

Her words hit the nail on the head with such accuracy that he looked away in case she could read his thoughts.

"It will make all the difference."

"No, sweet, it won't. I am the one you cherish in your heart, just as you live in mine. There are no walls high enough to keep us apart. Whatever you do, our love will withstand it and grow stronger because of it. It will all work out, you'll see. Meanwhile, don't fret. I shall be patient until you send for me."

She kissed him again and he couldn't prevent himself from responding, nor holding her slender body close to his, intoxicated by her perfume and the magic of her presence.

When she had gone he buried his head in his hands. He was very much afraid that she was right; it wasn't going to work. Marriage with Sapphire wouldn't affect the strange empathy which he and Minty felt for each other. Then he remembered how unlawful those tight bonds were and shuddered.

He would go on loving her until he drew his last breath, knowing she would be just as faithful. But somehow he had to escape from her in order to save her immortal soul.

He rose, feeling old at twenty-five.

Oh, God, Minty, he said under his breath, how on earth am I going to live without you? I wish you knew why I had to do this, and the reason for our parting, but I can't tell you. I'm not brave enough to watch your love turn to loathing.

Dearest, dearest Minty, I'm sorry, but that is something I just couldn't bear to see.

The news that FitzMaurice was going to marry Sapphire had spurred the earl on to making fresh enquiries about him. Ashton was so sure he was right about the nature of the man that he knew he had to move fast. He couldn't have Sapphire himself, but he wasn't going to let her fall into the hands of someone of Lyndon's calibre.

When he tried the men at Hatley again he had a piece of luck. Old Rob Sallows, who had been ill with bronchitis when Ashton had first asked questions, was back and helping with

148

the winch. He had known the Greys better than most, explaining that Mr and Mrs Grey and their son Percy were dead, but that Albert, Olive and Gladys lived just outside Pendlebury.

When Ashton arrived at their cottage they were awed by his presence, Olive quickly dusting a chair for his lordship to sit on. They hadn't a lot to tell him, bewildered by what he was asking them.

"What did he look like?"

Gladys was filling a chipped brown tea-pot from the kettle on the hob.

"Like most folk, I suppose. 'Ad a lot o' dark curls."

"What colour were his eyes?"

They looked at Stonehurst as if he were mad.

Finally, Olive said: "Well, brownish, I suppose."

"You're not sure?"

"Nay. Couldn't tell you colour o' Albert's eyes over there wi'out 'avin' another look."

It seemed incredible to Ashton that people could live hugger-mugger in a tiny cottage and not be aware of one another's appearance. He tried a different tack.

"Did you get on well with him?"

"Nay, 'e never 'ad much to do wi' rest of us." Gladys put a cup of tea down in front of Ashton which he hoped he could avoid drinking. "Allus on about gettin' learned."

"That's reet." Albert, crippled with arthritis at twenty, was hunched by the fire. "Many's a time our pa used to threaten 'im wi' stick if 'e didn't stop 'is nonsense."

"Yes, our Donald was a greet one for wantin' to better 'imself." Gladys sat at the table, sipping away. "Never forgot what 'e said to me one day, just afore 'e went. First off, 'e spoke in a foreign language and I could 'ave dropped in me boots."

Ashton glanced at her, prematurely old through drawing corves thirteen hours a day.

"What sort of foreign language?"

" 'Ee, I dunno. I asked 'im what it meant and 'e said: 'Remember to keep a calm mind i' difficulties.' Struck me so

149

funny, that's why I recalls it so well. 'Oo can keep mind calm when scratchin' around for food and coppers to pay t'rent?"

"Aequam memento rebus in arduis servare mentem."

They all turned their heads to stare at the earl in blank amazement. Then Albert spoke.

"What be that then, m'lord? Frenchie, is it, or mebbe Spanish?"

"Neither, it's Latin. Who would have taught your brother Latin, and perhaps other subjects as well?"

"Oh, that 'ud be Parson Grant. It were 'im Donald wanted to get lessons from, only Pa said we diddn't 'ave brass for it and neither did we."

"Yet somehow your brother must have got his own way. You don't learn Latin tags down a coal mine. But wouldn't you have known if he were going to the church regularly?"

"Not us. Donald were allus out o' an evenin'. 'E didn't say wheer 'e were goin' and we didn't ask."

Again Ashton felt some astonishment. It was a simple matter to avoid one's relatives in Lindborough Hall with its thirty bedrooms and countless reception rooms. Yet in a tiny miner's cottage, the Greys had lived and eaten and slept, seemingly unaware of what the others were doing, or what each member of the family looked like.

Olive was thoughtful.

"Come to think o' it, once or twice o' nights when I went out to t'—well—t'bottom o' garden, I saw a light from the old shed against the 'ouse. Could 'ave been Donald i' there, readin'."

The earl thanked them, surreptitiously leaving a few guineas on his chair. The Greys reeked of poverty and it made him ashamed of having so much.

He thought about the plaque in the vestry as he rode home, and of a pit-boy who had probably been well taught by the scholarly Grant, and who possibly spent the night hours devouring books instead of sleeping.

'Remember to keep a calm mind in difficulties'. The phrase could have been coined especially for FitzMaurice and Ashton could think of no man whose mind would be calmer in a crisis,

150

whatever the colour of his hair.

But guessing wasn't enough; he needed proof. First, that Donald Grey and Lyndon FitzMaurice were one and the same. Secondly, whether the accidents at Hatley had been caused on his instructions. Thirdly, if the latter were true, had it been merely a means of trying to buy the mine cheaply, or was there real malice involved? And, lastly, if malice there was, what was the reason for it?

Lyndon was said to have come from London where he had made his money. It might have been just idle gossip, but the City was the place where fortunes were made by clever men. Ashton had a number of friends in town, and his own lawyer and banker had offices in the heart of the capital.

The next move, therefore, was to go south and ask a few more questions and the sooner that was done the better.

One way or the other, FitzMaurice's marriage to Sapphire had to be stopped.

The wedding of Sapphire Grant and Lyndon FitzMaurice took place on a cheerless November day. The earl was still in London, unaware that the banns had been read three times and all other formalities dealt with.

The church was full, for the locals dearly liked a wedding, the women exclaiming over Sapphire's crimson gown and soft furs. Lyndon was thankful that Minty hadn't come. It was hard enough as it was to stand in front of the altar with Sapphire. If Minty had been in the congregation, he thought he would have turned and run before the moment came for the ring to be slipped on to his bride's finger.

When the jollifications were over, Sapphire went to the room in Deerpark Manor which had been prepared for her. She knew nothing about Lord Roger, and gave credit to her new husband for the excellent taste shewn in the decorations and draperies.

They had decided not to go away; a honeymoon would have been a farce in the circumstances. As Sapphire undressed and got into bed she didn't know how she was going to survive the next few hours. It wasn't that she was facing the unknown; she knew Lyndon only too well. It was the thought of making love to another man, when she had almost reached heaven in Ashton's arms, which made her tremble.

It was an hour before FitzMaurice knocked on her door. Sapphire had almost given him up for lost, and was beginning to relax. Then he was there, walking to the end of the bed and looking at her in a way he had never done before.

For a while the silence held. Sapphire could see sorrow in FitzMaurice and another emotion, deeper and more dreadful. She said quietly: "What is it, Lyndon? Is something wrong?"

He seemed to come out of a reverie, moving to the side of the bed.

"May I sit here?"

She nodded, more perplexed than ever. His request was humbly put, as if he expected it to be refused. After a moment or two he said tiredly: "I can't sleep with you tonight."

Sapphire tried not to shew her relief, waiting for him to continue.

"I can never make love to you, but as compensation I'll tell you a story. It isn't a pretty one. Indeed, it's exceedingly ugly, but I've lived with it on my own for too long. Now that you're my wife, I can share my secret with you, if not my bed."

His eyes looked blind and he seemed to be lost for the words he needed.

"I'm a good listener," said Sapphire gently. "Everyone says so."

He gave a faint smile.

"Yes, I expect you are and, if I have to explain this dark thing inside me to someone, I'm glad it's to you."

Once started, Lyndon's tale flowed as swiftly as the stream where he used to wash himself when he was a boy. He began with his first day as a trapper in Hatley Mine, leaving nothing out and finishing with his hopeless passion for Arminta Howard and what he had done to her.

Sapphire leaned back against the pillows, temporarily paralysed. She tried not to condemn or lash out at him because

152

she'd been made a tool to end his *affaire*. She waited until she was calmer before she spoke, Lyndon apparently unaware of the leaden silence which had fallen again.

In the end, Sapphire said unsteadily: "But Minty's your half-sister. Lyndon, don't you realise what—?"

"Of course I realise what it is. It's incest, but Minty doesn't know that. She is innocent of any sin; it is I who have committed this gross offence. I wanted to marry you so that I had to keep away from her."

"You'll have to." Sapphire was very sharp. "Whatever happens, you must never see Minty again. What you've already done is so dreadful that I'm sickened by it, but it must end here."

"Will you help me?"

"I've no choice."

"How I must disgust you."

Sapphire was on the point of assuring him that he most certainly did, when suddenly she thought of Ashton. If Ashton had been her half-brother would she still have fallen in love with him, or been able to deny him if he'd wanted her? She knew the answer at once, beginning to see behind FitzMaurice's crime the strength of his obsession for Arminta Howard.

Human beings didn't get the chance to choose the one they loved. It just happened, and the gods had made cruel sport of Lyndon.

"No," she said, her voice softer. "No, you don't. I shouldn't have said what I did just now. I know how difficult it is to—"

"You love Ashton, don't you? I've always known that and realised he must feel the same. As I told you, that was another reason for wanting to make you my wife and why I raped you that day. I couldn't hit back at my father; he was dead. Ashton had to suffer in his place and I punished him through you. I'm sorry, and thank you for your understanding. I don't deserve it. I think we'd better go back to London as soon as I've cleared up certain matters here. Then perhaps we can travel. Your family's in Rome, isn't it? I'll take you to see your mother. I really will do my best to make it up to you."

"And Minty?"

He gave a deep sigh.

"Minty said she would wait for me. That's why I have to get away in a week or two."

"Can't we go at once? Tomorrow?"

"No, that's not possible. I must attend to some business first."

"But you promise not to see Minty?"

He met her worried eyes and raised his hands helplessly.

"I can promise to try not to; beyond that I cannot go."

"Lyndon! This is insanity."

"I know, I know. Don't you think I realise that? She fills my mind every moment of the day; at night she walks in my dreams. She's in my blood and in my heart, and she's never going to let me go."

He saw the tears on Sapphire's cheeks and gently wiped them away.

"Don't cry. I'll do my best, but I'm not going to lie to you. I don't know whether I can fight her."

"You'll have to. Together we must win this battle."

"Poor Sapphire." He put his hand over hers. "Your share of the bargain hasn't turned out too well, I'm afraid. At least I've got old Broom's mine out of this."

"I was going to have a lot of fun tonight telling you about Bluehill. Now it doesn't seem to be of any importance."

He looked up.

"Fun? What sort of fun?"

Sapphire told him of the codicil, waiting for anger to take the place of grief. Instead, he stared at her for a minute and then started to laugh.

"Splendid, Mrs FitzMaurice, quite splendid! You're a woman after my own heart. I congratulate you, and Broom, too. He's won, hasn't he? The first time I saw him I told myself I shouldn't underestimate him but, in the end, I fell into that oldest trap of all. I hope he's enjoying his triumph, wherever his is; he deserves to. Goodnight, my dear, and try to forgive

154

me if you can."

Sapphire blew out her candle and turned on her side, convinced that she would get no sleep that night. But in the end, when dawn was touching the sky with hazy pink fingers, slumber took pity on her. Her last conscious thought was for the earl.

"Ashton," she whispered as her eyes began to close, "we were right. Minty did need to be watched over, but we didn't do a very good job, I'm afraid. Oh, my darling, my darling, we failed. We failed!"

TEN

Ashton's return home was delayed. He felt that every hour away from Sapphire counted and he wanted to get back to her as soon as possible. He was on the point of departure when Portia, Marchioness of Mildensey, arrived at his London house. Portia was a formidable woman, Ashton's paternal aunt and the scourge of the family. The prospect of telling her to go away was one at which even the earl balked, not least because he knew she would ignore him.

He consoled himself with the information which his banker, Charles Walraven, had given him. Lyndon FitzMaurice, it seemed, was extremely well-known in financial circles. He was also heartily disliked because of his youth, his outstanding success, and his lack of respect for the elder statesmen of the Stock Exchange.

"I only met him once," said Walraven, when Ashton dined with him. "Striking feller and clever as Old Nick. He was Raymond Betteridge's protegée, you know. Taught Fitz-Maurice all he knew and left him all he possessed. Story goes that FitzMaurice once saved Raymond from some thieves; that's how they met."

"What else is known about him?"

Charles shrugged.

"Apart from his business acumen and incredible luck, not much."

"Surely there's something. This isn't idle curiosity, Walraven. I really need to know."

The banker cocked an eyebrow at Stonehurst.

"Mm, you do, don't you? Well, the only other thing I can recall is what Betteridge said to me one night when he was in his cups. He told me that FitzMaurice had come from Lancashire as a mere stripling. Said he wanted to make a lot of money and then return home to right a great wrong done to him."

Ashton felt as if the answer to the conundrum was almost in the palm of his hand.

"Lancashire? What sort of wrong?"

"Raymond didn't know. FitzMaurice was very tight-mouthed about whatever it was."

During the journey north, the earl had time to think. White hair or not, he knew now beyond any doubt that Donald Grey and Lyndon FitzMaurice were the same person; everything fitted. What he didn't know, but had to find out as swiftly as he could, was the nature of the wrong which Lyndon felt he had to put right.

Grey had worked at Hatley, so it was quite possible that some incident had occurred there which had turned him against his employer. Many miners harboured resentment against the mine owners, but not all men were like Fitz-Maurice. If the Howard family had offended, how were they to be punished? For some reason the thought of Minty came into Ashton's mind and a frisson ran through him as if he had been touched by the hand of death.

Ashton was soon told of Sapphire's marriage and his heart sank. He was too late, and cursed himself for not finding out how far arrangements had gone before he left. Then he realised that even if had known every last detail, he wouldn't have been able to do anything. Sapphire wouldn't listen to him after their last encounter and clearly FitzMaurice was unyielding in his purpose. He had wanted Bluehill and now he had got it.

Ashton had only been back a day or two when he met Sapphire. She had gone riding alone, refusing to take a maid or groom with her. She felt as if she were in a prison cell and wanted solitude to consider the future she was facing. The earl's ride was taken for much the same reason. He didn't want to talk to anyone; he needed to be by himself to work things out and try to guess what Lyndon's next move would be.

When he saw Sapphire he felt a spasm of real fear. She was very pale and drawn and as they walked over to each other he could see the despair in her eyes.

"Sapphire? What is it? You're like a ghost."

"It's nothing. I've had a slight chill, but I'm over it now."

"I don't believe you. A chill wouldn't make you look like that. Is FitzMaurice ill-treating you?"

"Of course not."

She tried to put conviction into her voice, but the memory of what Lyndon had told her made her denial sound false. Her husband hadn't physically abused her, but what he had done was worse than a hundred blows. She was also worried about Minty. Lyndon hadn't given her his oath that he would stay away from his half-sister; he had merely said he would try to do so. The possibility that Minty and Lyndon might at that very moment be together was too horrible to contemplate.

Gently, Ashton took her in his arms. There was no passion this time, merely the comforting embrace of an old friend.

"You're too brave, my darling," he said quietly. "I know if I questioned you for an hour or more you'd still insist that nothing was wrong. Give me your word on one thing."

It was wonderful to be close to Ashton again and Sapphire wanted to lay her head on his breast and let the whole sordid tale be given freedom. But she couldn't speak of it, particularly to him.

"What thing?" she said sadly. "Don't ask too much of me, for I haven't got it to give."

"I won't. Just promise me that if the situation gets too bad you'll come to me. Please, my love, say that you will."

She nodded. The present state of affairs couldn't get much worse and her vow need only be a vague one to pacify him.

"Yes, I'll come to you," she said as their eyes met again in mutual longing. "When it gets more than I can bear, I'll tell you. Dear Ashton; thank you for being here this morning. I thought I wanted to be alone, but I was wrong. One can have a bit too much of loneliness, don't you think?"

"I couldn't stay away from you after all."

"I knew you wouldn't be able to. That's why I said I'd wait for you."

Lyndon and Minty sat in the far corner of the chapel, she in a sable-lined cloak, he in a heavy greatcoat to keep out the biting winds. She hadn't been surprised to get Lyndon's note, delivered with a knowing look and slight giggles by Miss Thornley. Lela said that a boy had given it to her and hadn't demurred at the prospect of a chilly wait. She had found herself a niche in the vestry, well away from her mistress, her hands tucked into a fur muff which Minty had given her as a gift.

"Minty, there's something I've got to tell you. It will end our meetings for good, but you must be told the truth."

She smiled as she let her hood fall back. Her curls were powdered with snow and Lyndon thought she looked more than ever like a vision from a fairy tale. He had tried so hard to keep his promise to Sapphire, but it had proved impossible. He had to see Minty just once more, even if it meant losing her in a dreadful way. He was prepared for their parting now; it was the only way to save her.

"Nothing will end our meetings."

"You don't know what I'm going to say."

"It doesn't matter what it is; it can't separate us. The bonds between us are too strong."

He looked at her sombrely as she gave him his cue.

"That's the trouble, they are not only too strong, they are

159

also unlawful."

She met his eyes, giving him encouragement to go on.

"Unlawful? My darling, how can they be?"

"Very easily. Minty, I'm your father's bastard and thus your brother. Incest is not only illegal, it's vile. There's no way I can explain why I let it happen. I set out to crucify Stonehurst because he had turned me away when I was born and wouldn't acknowledge me as his son. I raped Sapphire Grant because I knew Ashton loved her. That was my first blow against your family. You were next on my list, to be dealt with in the same way as Sapphire. Then I saw you at Broom's party and my whole life changed in a single moment.

"One of your father's servants saw us in the wood. Stonehurst came to see me, raging like a mad bull because of the violation of his daughter. I told him the truth and it killed him. I followed him back to the Hall. If he hadn't died that way, I would have murdered him to stop him talking. I would have protected you in any way I could. I paid off the servant, threatening him with death if he opened his mouth or returned to Lancashire. Now do you see why this has to finish?"

"I always knew there was more than ordinary mortal love between us," Minty said softly. "There had to be, because of the way I felt about you, and you about me. I see the reason now. We are bound together by common blood as well as desire."

He stared at her, unable to believe what she was saying.

"Minty, do you know what I've been talking about? Do you understand what incest is?"

Her laughter was like music in the icy chapel.

"Dearest, of course I do, and yes, I know exactly what you've been saying."

"But—but aren't you shocked? I expected you to recoil in abhorrence; to shrink away from me in revulsion."

"It is you who weren't listening." Minty laid a hand on his cheek. "I said I'd known from the start that we were not as others are. Lyndon, this makes no difference to me, nor must it trouble you."

160

"But think what I've done and what else I was prepared to do. Your father's death—Sapphire—I married her because I thought she might keep me away from you."

"I know, you explained. I told you then that there were no walls high enough to separate us."

"I'm bestial—diseased."

"You are my love."

"Oh, God, Minty, don't make it so easy for me. Tell me to go away and never trouble you again."

She shook her head.

"It will all work out in the end; I said that, too."

"But if we keep meeting I shan't be able to stop myself from making love to you. As you lie in my arms, you'll know I'm your kin—your brother."

"My half-brother and of course you will make love to me. That's why I came today."

"You are too forgiving; it's wrong."

"I'm not in the least forgiving. There's nothing to pardon. I wasn't sure what made me feel so much a part of you, but I knew there had to be something. I didn't care what it was then, and I don't care now."

"You should, you should! Minty, what are you doing?"

"Undressing, at least, disrobing sufficiently for what we both know we have to do."

"No! Go, go! For pity's sake turn and run."

"Put your hands on my body, hold me close to you, touch my lips with yours, and then tell me to go."

He was like a man in a trance as obediently he stretched out his arms. Her skin was satin-smooth and cold and he knew he had to warm her. When their mouths met he realised that she'd won.

He put her cloak down to protect them from the stone-flags as they came together with greater passion than ever before.

When they were dressed again, Lyndon held Minty's hand in his, rubbing her fingers so that the frost shouldn't cause her too much discomfort.

He was very matter-of-fact as he gave her a quick smile.

161

"My beloved, there is only one place for us and it isn't in this world."

She leaned against him, full of contentment.

"No, I know that, but at least we shall be together for always."

"Yes, we will. Tomorrow we'll make the arrangements. Will you come here at the same time?"

"Of course. Now I had better go and find poor old Lela. She hasn't got anything but a muff to protect her from the weather. We are luckier."

"Give me one more kiss before you go, sweet."

It was a long one and, for the first time since he'd met her, Lyndon was truly at peace. Minty had washed away his guilt, his fears, his self-hatred, and every other ill. All that was left was his love for her.

"Tomorrow," she whispered as she turned to go. "At the same time."

"Tomorrow."

The word echoed through the empty building, still hanging in the air after she had disappeared. But there wasn't to be a tomorrow for Lyndon FitzMaurice.

When he reached Deerpark Manor, servants rushed out to tell him of a disaster at Elstone. Without stopping to think, he turned and rode hell for leather to the mine, leaping out of the saddle and demanding to know what had happened.

On the south side a part of the roof had caved in and there was the threat of flooding. Already water was beginning to trickle in sinister fashion along the narrow tunnels.

"How many trapped?" asked FitzMaurice curtly. "And where are they?"

" 'Bout twenty, sir. They be in section next to disused workin's, where water's comin' from. 'Ad to be closed years back 'cos it couldn't be pumped dry. A sort o' dam were built 'tween it and rest of long-face, but we all knew it wouldn't last for ever. No 'ope of gettin' 'em out."

"Why not?"

"Too much to move to set 'em free. Afore we'd finished, the

162

rest o' t'old part 'ud give way, dam an' all."

"I'm going in." Lyndon took off his coat and waistcoat. "Any of you who want to help, follow me. If you don't feel like risking your necks, stay where you are."

A dozen men with candles crawled in after him, moved by the concern he had shown for their companions, and his willingness to forfeit his own life. The group worked like maniacs, pulling coal and wood away, ignoring the remaining props which moaned and creaked with renewed threats. They could feel their feet growing wetter and wetter as finally a hole was made, just large enough for FitzMaurice to get through.

"Wait here," he ordered. "I'll hand the survivors out to you. Be ready, and be quick to get them away. There's not much time left."

Lyndon didn't stop to consider the danger he was in. Minty would have wanted him to save as many lives as he could and he went to work with a will.

The first four or five were easy to get through the gap; then things got harder. Lyndon strained every muscle and sinew as he lifted great lumps of rock and timber from the backs of those pinned down, half-dragging them to where the others waited to haul them to safety. A few were already dead and he didn't waste energy on them. It was the living who mattered.

He had just got the tenth victim out when the sound came which he'd been dreading. The old workings had finally collapsed completely. The distant rumble warned of what was coming and he threw a boy to the waiting rescuers. He was just reaching for a girl, half-covered by a strut, when he heard the torrent on its way.

"Run!" he shouted to the miners whose faces were like spectres in the dim light. "Run like hell; it's too late for any more. Shovel as much as you can into this hole. It might stem the water long enough for you to get away."

"Maister, you'll be buried alive!"

"I'll be drowned, you fool. Get on with it, for Christ's sake. You've got split seconds, not hours."

The gap began to close as four of the workers feverishly

placed rocks, coal, timber and anything else which they could find into the opening. They rammed the packing home with steel fists to keep it in place for as long as possible. Then, at last, they obeyed FitzMaurice and scuttled back along the tunnel at a speed they'd never achieved before.

Lyndon only had time to turn his head before the end came. The maelstrom was like a giant beast as it flung itself against the make-shift barrier, surging back to sweep up everything in its path. It wouldn't be long before it broke through the rubble; meanwhile it claimed as many souls as it could in its savage fury.

At the surface everyone was talking of what FitzMaurice had done. Disasters were commonplace; death an everyday event. A colliery owner sacrificing his own life for others was rare, and the miners pulled off their caps in a spontaneous tribute to the man they had once disliked most heartily.

"Never 'ad much time for 'im," said one. "This'll teach me not to judge so quick, like."

"Aye, I thought 'e were a wrong 'un from t'start. Shows 'ee can't allus tell."

An overseer summed up the sentiments of them all as he watched the injured being carried away.

"You never said a truer word, Jim; can't allus tell and that's a fact. Whatever 'e did afore this don't matter now. At t'last 'e were reet champion. Can't say better o' anyone 'un that, can 'ee?"

"She's gone, Toby."

"I know. Tom Bailey were by 'ere not long since."

Tobias Locket still couldn't believe that Essie Gosling was dead. He had shouted at her early that morning when she'd called by with a loaf and some tea, telling her he didn't want her charity. She'd ignored his spleen, laying the things on the table and promising to see him that night. He's spat his anger at her, warning her not to show her face. He loved her as much as ever, but he had to keep her at bay with false rancour. She was beginning to soften him up, and they both knew it. Then Essie would be saddled with him for good; a man with a trunk, a head and two arms. He couldn't let it happen to her, but the fight got harder every day.

Normally, Birdie Locket never sat down during the day. She always claimed she'd far too much to do to be so idle. That morning it was different, and she leaned back in her rocker, her lips no longer pinched with spite.

"Didn't used to like 'er, but 'course you knew that. Thought she might 'urt you more 'un you'd been 'urt already, leadin' you on wi' promises. I gave 'er the length of me tongue many a time; wish I 'adn't now. She were a good lass; I could see that after a while. She didn't 'ave to come 'ere bringin' us food and such-like."

Toby closed his eyes, seeing Essie's snub nose, wide smile and eyes like precious stones.

"No, she didn't, but I'm more to blame than you, Ma, for 'ow she were treated under this roof. No reason why you should 'ave been civil to 'er, I suppose. Was different for me. You see, I loved 'er."

"I know." Mrs Locket began to rock backwards and forwards, needing to be on the go, even in her chair. "And she felt t'same about you."

"She did, but all she got out o' me were curses."

"Doubt if she took notice of 'em."

"Why shouldn't she? I swore at 'er somethin' terrible."

"If she'd thought you'd really gone off 'er, she wouldn't 'ave kept comin'."

"You don't think so?"

Birdie heard the plea in her son's voice, quick to build on his hope.

"Nay, 'course not. What lass in 'er right senses would? She saw through you, lad, never fear. Sharp as a packet of needles, were Essie Gosling. Wish I'd been able to say one kind word afore this 'appened."

"And I wish I'd been man enough to tell 'er there wasn't no other girl in t'world for me."

"She didn't need tellin'. Likes I said, she knew. It 'ud 'ave

165

been quick, Toby, wouldn't it? She wouldn't 'ave—"

"Tom said at end it were quick enough. Last thing 'e saw were Mr FitzMaurice tryin' to pull 'er free. Then maister told 'em to fill up t'ole and get away. Only just did it in time, seemingly. Tom said 'e never saw men move so fast in all 'is born days. They got out; t'rest were drowned."

"Don't upset 'eself, Toby; she be well enough now."

"She may be, but I'm not. Last thing I said to 'er was that she were a schemin' whore. Oh, Jesus, Ma, I said she were an whore and now I'll not set eyes on 'er again."

Toby turned his face to the wall and began to cry. After a while Birdie got up and knelt beside her son, pulling him into her arms as she used to do when he was a baby.

"There, there, luv. I'm a disagreeable old faggot and I knows it, but you've still got me. Ain't the same as Essie, I'll grant you, but it's better 'un nothin', ain't it?"

Toby's sobs had died down and he looked up at his mother. He would never forgive himself, but life had to go on somehow.

"Aye," he said, and tried to give Birdie a smile. "Anythin's better 'un nowt. We'll 'ave to make do wi' one another, won't we?"

"That we will and we'll manage. 'Ave to learn to crack me face more often and find a job. Now, 'ow about me makin' you a strong cup o' tea? If Essie were 'ere, that's what she'd tell me to do."

"You reckon?"

"Certain of it. Sensible lass, she were. We'll drink one, special for 'er, shall we?"

Toby wiped his eyes with the back of his hand and nodded.

"Aye, 'specially for 'er. Thanks, Ma; I'd like that fine."

It was Ashton who told Minty of Lyndon's death. The expression on her face didn't change as she murmured cool regrets.

She listened to the tale of FitzMaurice's unflinching valour and Ashton's praise of it. She was glad that Lyndon had done something he would be remembered by. So many died and no

166

one ever gave them a second's thought after they were buried. Those Lyndon had saved would be a kind of memorial to him and she almost smiled, because she knew he would have roared with laughter at such an idea.

"I'll go and see Sapphire tomorrow," she said as she began to mount the stairs to her room. "I don't think we should disturb her today, do you? I'll write her a note and have it taken to the Manor."

Ashton wanted to get to Sapphire as quickly as he could, but perhaps Minty was right. She always seemed to sense what other people needed and probably Sapphire would be glad of a few hours on her own.

At one o'clock in the morning, Minty left Lindborough Hall as quietly as a mouse. She wore the cloak on which she and Lyndon had lain not long before, carrying a lantern in one hand.

It was freezing cold, snow and ice underfoot, but she didn't notice that. It took quite a long time to get to the log where she and Lyndon used to sit, but neither the elements nor the darkness halted her progress.

When at last she reached the place where they had held each other and spoken of love, the log had vanished under a snowdrift. That wasn't important either, for Minty knew exactly where it had been.

She put her lantern down and smiled.

"You're here, darling, aren't you? I can feel you close to me. I'm sorry I wasn't with you at Elstone. You were so courageous and everyone is talking about what you did. They'll always remember that you gave your life to save others."

She drew one of Ashton's pistols from under her cloak, giving a slight laugh.

"Wasn't it a good thing that Father taught me how to use one of these? He said such skills might be of help to me one day, and he was right. I always enjoyed shooting practice much more than sewing or playing the piano."

The gale howled dismally through the shorn trees, trying to knock her over with its force, but nothing could alter her chosen course. She had already loaded the gun and everything was ready.

"I wish I could have got here before, but I had to wait until everyone was in bed. How the hours dragged for me; was it the same for you?"

She removed her hood, sad that what she was about to do would hurt Ashton and Sapphire, but it couldn't be helped. She still cared deeply for them, but she had to follow Lyndon to another place where they could be at peace.

"Wait for me, Lyndon, won't you?" she said softly. "I'm coming now. My dearest, how very, very lucky we have been. As I said once before, I've no idea what we did to deserve such blessings, but perhaps I'll know in a few minutes' time. If I don't find the answer, I shan't worry.

"You'll be there to take me in your arms again, won't you, and that is all which will ever matter to me."

When Sapphire heard that Minty had been found by two boys collecting firewood she went straight to Lindborough Hall. She was shown into the drawing-room where Ashton was standing with a letter in his hand.

"It's from Allene," he said dully. "It seems she's found a French marquis she wants to marry. Thank God for that. Sapphire, why did Minty do it? I don't understand. I thought she was happy; she seemed to be. When I said goodnight to her she kissed me as she always did and told me to sleep tight. There was nothing different about her."

Sapphire had been trying for the last half-hour to find a way to tell Ashton the truth. She had been oddly moved by Lyndon's death, although she hadn't loved him. He had died heroically and she knew what had made him give up his life for the trapped workers. When she had first met him he wouldn't have lifted a finger to aid them, but Minty had changed him in more ways than one. Sapphire had witnessed the first softening of him some time before she had married him, but hadn't known the reason for it then.

"I know why."

168

The earl had been looking into the fire, but he turned quickly as she spoke.

"You do?"

"Yes, she wrote me a letter."

"Of condolence."

"More than that."

The earl was very white round the mouth.

"Are you saying you were aware of her intention to kill herself and did nothing about it?"

"Ashton! No, of course not. I had no idea she was going to take her own life, but I understand why she did. It's a terrible story, but I suppose you ought to be told."

He was curt.

"Certainly I should. If you know why Minty took a gun, put it to her temple, and then pulled the trigger, in the name of Almighty God, tell me."

She did so, as gently and as concisely as she could. When her voice died away the earl was the colour of wax.

"She found out that Lyndon was her half-brother, yet she still continued the *affaire*?"

"Yes, I told you. In her note she explained that Lyndon had made a full confession. It made no difference to her."

"Dear God! Now all my questions are answered. I'd have been better off left in ignorance as to why FitzMaurice bore such a grudge against my family. I know what shocked my father and caused his heart attack. I know, too, whom he wanted me to save. It was Minty, after all, although he didn't speak her name. Perhaps he couldn't do so, after what he'd just heard.

"I told you long ago I feared Minty was walking towards some kind of danger and that in the end I wouldn't be able to save her."

"She didn't want to be saved," Sapphire said quietly. "She wanted to be with Lyndon."

Ashton looked sick, and Sapphire's heart went out to him. She had had some time to come to terms with the situation; he hadn't.

169

"I still can't take it in," he went on, his fingers locked tightly together. "She looked so pure, so innocent. She wore a mask of sweetness, but behind that was this evil corruption. How could she? Minty, of all people, embroiled in something so depraved, so unspeakably unnatural. I always thought of her as a child."

"But she wasn't a child. She was a woman, deeply in love. And it didn't seem evil to them. That was clear from Minty's letter. What they felt for each other was so powerful that it rose above man-made laws."

"And God's laws."

"Yes, God's laws as well, but even that didn't matter to them. Lyndon felt guilt at first, but Minty washed that away for him. When he told me the whole story on our wedding night, I felt just as you do now. Afterwards, I had time to think. I'm not condoning what they did; I just think I understand it a little better, that's all. I hope it may be the same for you in the end."

"Accept that my sister knowingly had an incestuous relationship with our half-brother and then committed suicide?"

"Yes, for that is what happened and nothing you can do will change the facts. You cared for her so much, Ashton. Go on caring for the girl you knew."

"I'm not sure that I can."

"I'm going to give you another shock."

He raised his head to look at her.

"I doubt if you can. I feel dead, as dead as Minty is."

"Nevertheless, I'm going to try. After I'd listened to Lyndon, judging him as you're doing now, I stopped to ask myself a question. If you were my half-brother, would I still have fallen in love with you and become your mistress, if you'd let me?"

It seemed a long time before the earl spoke again and Sapphire was holding her breath.

"Well?" he enquired finally. "How did you answer yourself?"

"With a free admission that I would be in love with you for all my life, whatever our relationship was, and that I would share

170

your bed without shame. That is how much I want you. It was how much Minty and Lyndon needed each other."

Ashton looked back at his hands.

"I'd like to go riding up on the moor for about an hour. I need to be alone and in silence. Is it too much to ask you to stay here until I get back?"

Sapphire shook her head.

"Not too much at all. I'll wait for you."

When the earl returned, Sapphire was admiring a collection of china ornaments by the window.

"This reminds me of my visits to Mrs Sheldon. I was always looking around, fascinated by her things. She didn't mind; she knew I liked beautiful objects."

"Beauty attracts beauty. What will you do now?"

She turned from the side-table, joining him by the fire.

"Go to Rome for a few months. When I was small, and unhappy, I used to climb on to my mother's lap and cry against her shoulder. I need that shoulder again."

Ashton had forced his nightmare aside for a while. The desolate moor, the uncaring wind, and the solitude had numbed him. He looked at Sapphire and managed a smile.

"You're as slender as a wand, but aren't you a bit too heavy for your mother's lap?"

"She'll manage; you don't know Megan. And you?"

"I'll go to Somerset. I've got another estate there. The house is small, but quite perfect and there are too many ghosts here."

Sapphire said casually: "I shall come back in June. Will you be here then?"

"Do you want me to be?"

He longed to pour out his love for her, she praying that he would.

"You know I do. How can we be married if I'm in Rome and you're in Somerset?"

That time he was even able to give a laugh.

"You brazen hussy. What makes you think I want to marry you?"

"Because, in spite of the fact that you're a nobleman and I'm

171

a humble vicar's daughter, I remember what it was like in my bedroom that afternoon. That was what mattered, not our social status."

"I can remember it, too." He searched her face, hoping his next question wouldn't spoil the fragile thread they held between them. "Sapphire, how can you want me after all this? I know what you said before I went out, but my family's tainted."

"And mine was very poor. What has either thing got to do with us? Is our love less than Lyndon's and Minty's? Look what they did, just to be together."

"No, it's not less than theirs."

"Then don't be foolish. Do you want an empty, barren life, brooding over something which is finished?"

"Of course not, but—"

"Neither do I. I want a husband, a lover, and a father for all the children I'm going to have."

The earl felt the ice in his veins begin to thaw, his head clearing.

"Not too many, I hope. You'll never have any time for me with a dozen infants round your skirts."

"They won't all be infants at the same time. There were five of us, yet my mother and father were in love until the day he died. Megan knew how to be both wife and mother, and I'm her daughter. But we can discuss later the exact number we're going to have."

"Next summer?"

"Yes. I'll send word to you when I return."

"And I'll ask you to meet me in the wood where we used to go."

"And I shall write a note saying I will be there."

"Then I'll hold your hand in mine."

Sapphire moved nearer to Ashton.

"That's all right while we are in the wood, but next time we're in a bedroom together I shall expect a good deal more than that. I haven't quite forgiven you for the last time."

He put his arms round her, knowing that only she could cure his wounds and make him whole again.

172

"I haven't forgotten either, but you needn't worry. I never make the same mistake twice. Dearest Sapphire, if you weren't here I don't think I'd want to go on living."

"But I am here, so don't be morbid. If you intend to go on looking backwards, why are you holding me so tightly?"

"Because I can't find the words to tell you what you mean to me."

"Words don't matter. For goodness' sake, Ashton, haven't you any imagination?"

"Oh, yes," he said softly and bent to touch her waiting lips. "I'll show you just how much when we meet again. Meanwhile, will this do to go on with?"

Sapphire was breathless when he let her go, full of ecstasy and hope. She hadn't been sure if she could pull him out of his dark abyss, but in the end it had been all right.

"Yes, that will do for the moment," she said sedately. "Indeed, it will do very well for the time being."

Then she laughed aloud and give him a hug, mischief dancing in her eyes.

"Ashton."

"Sweetheart?"

"Isn't it a pity that June is so far off? And I've changed my mind. That was very enjoyable, but I'm afraid it won't be enough to keep me going until them. Darling, darling Ashton. Would you mind giving me just one more kiss?"